DISCOVERING CAREERS FOR YOUR FUTURE

publishing

Ferguson
An imprint of ✓® Facts On File

Discovering Careers for Your Future: Publishing

Copyright © 2005 by Facts On File, Inc.

All rights reserved. No part of this book may be reproduced or utilized in any form or by any means, electronic or mechanical, including photocopying, recording, or by any information storage or retrieval systems, without permission in writing from the publisher. For information contact

Ferguson
An imprint of Facts On File, Inc.
132 West 31st Street
New York NY 10001

Discovering careers for your future. Publishing.
    p. cm.
Includes bibliographical references and index.
    ISBN 0-8160-5845-8 (acid-free paper)
  1. Book industries and trade—Vocational guidance—United States—Juvenile literature. 2. Publishers and publishing—Vocational guidance—United States—Juvenile literature. 3. Printing industry—Vocational guidance—United States—Juvenile literature. 4. Authorship—Vocational guidance—United States—Juvenile literature. 5. Editing—Vocational guidance—United States—Juvenile literature. I. Facts On File, Inc.
  Z471.D57 2005
  070.5'.023'73—dc22   2004012837

Ferguson books are available at special discounts when purchased in bulk quantities for businesses, associations, institutions, or sales promotions. Please call our Special Sales Department in New York at (212) 967-8800 or (800) 322-8755.

You can find Ferguson on the World Wide Web at http://www.fergpubco.com

Text design by Mary Susan Ryan-Flynn

Printed in the United States of America

EB FOF 10 9 8 7 6 5 4 3 2 1

This book is printed on acid-free paper.

Contents

Introduction 1
Advertising and Marketing Workers 5
Art Directors 9
Bindery Workers 13
Book Editors 17
Columnists 21
Desktop Publishing Specialists 25
Graphic Designers 29
Illustrators 33
Indexers 37
Literary Agents 41
Magazine Editors 45
Newspaper Editors 49
Photographers 53
Prepress Workers 57
Printing Press Workers 61
Reporters 65
Science and Medical Writers 69
Technical Writers and Editors 73
Webmasters 77
Writers 81
Glossary 85
Index of Job Titles 89
Browse and Learn More 91

Introduction

You may not have decided yet what you want to be in the future. And you do not have to decide right away. You do know that right now you are interested in reading, writing, reporting, and design. Do any of the statements below describe you? If so, you may want to begin thinking about what a publishing career might mean for you.

___I love to read.
___I like to write.
___I enjoy surfing the Web.
___I enjoy computer-design programs.
___I like being the manager of school clubs.
___I keep a daily journal.
___I love to draw.
___I like to take photographs.
___I like to write about my opinions.
___I enjoy reading about science and medicine.
___I like to tell people about books and magazines and performers that I enjoy.
___I like to make up stories.
___I am interested in how books are made.
___I am curious about people and places.
___I like building websites.
___I ask a lot of questions.
___I am good at observing and describing small details.
___I read newspapers and magazines regularly.
___I like languages.
___I am a good speller.

Discovering Careers for Your Future: Publishing is a book about careers in the publishing industry, from advertising and marketing workers to book editors to writers. You can find careers in this field at publishing companies, in art studios, in business offices, and at printing companies. Although the publishing industry is centered in New York, publishing workers are employed throughout the United States and the world.

This book describes many possibilities for future careers related to publishing. Read through it and see how different careers are connected. For example, if you are interested in writing, you will want to read the chapters on columnists, science and medical writers, technical writers and editors, and other careers. If you are interested in editing, you will want to read the chapters on book editors, magazine editors, newspaper editors, and other careers. If you are more interested in arts-related careers, read the chapters on art directors, graphic designers, illustrators, and other careers. If you are interested in the actual process of printing books, you will want to read the chapters on bindery workers and printing press workers.

What Do Publishing Workers Do?

The first section of each chapter begins with a heading such as "What Photographers Do" or "What Writers Do." It tells what it is like to work at this job. It describes typical responsibilities and assignments. You will find out about working conditions. Would you work in an office all day? Would you have contact with lots of people? What tools and equipment would you use? This section answers all these questions.

How Do I Become a Publishing Worker?

The section called "Education and Training" tells you what schooling you need for employment in each job—a high school diploma, training at a junior college, a college degree, or perhaps more. It also talks about on-the-job training that you could expect to receive after you are hired and whether or not you must complete an apprenticeship program.

How Much Do Publishing Workers Earn?

The "Earnings" section gives the average salary figures for the job described in the chapter. These figures provide you with a general idea of how much money people with this job can make. Keep in mind that many people really earn more or less than the amounts given here because actual salaries depend on many different things, such as the size of the company, the location of the company, and the amount of education, training, and experience you have. Generally, but not always, bigger companies located in major cities pay more than smaller ones in smaller cities and towns, and people with more education, training, and experience earn more. Also remember that these figures are current or recent averages. They will probably be different by the time you are ready to enter the workforce.

What Is the Future of Publishing Careers?

The "Outlook" section discusses the employment outlook for the career: whether the total number of people employed in this career will increase or decrease in the coming years and whether jobs in this field will be easy or hard to find. These predictions are based on economic conditions, the size and makeup of the population, foreign competition, and new technology. Keep in mind that these predictions are general statements. No one knows for sure what the future will be like. Also remember that the employment outlook is a general statement about an industry and does not necessarily apply to everyone. A determined and talented person may be able to find a job in an industry or career with the worst kind of outlook. And a person without ambition and the proper training will find it difficult to find a job in even a booming industry or career field.

Where Can I Find More Information?

Each chapter concludes with a "For More Info" section. It lists resources that you can contact to find out more about the field and careers in the field. You will find the names, addresses, phone numbers, and websites of publishing-oriented associations and organizations.

Extras

Every chapter has a few extras. There are photos that show publishing workers in action. There are sidebars and notes on ways to explore the field, fun facts, profiles of people in the field, or lists of websites and books that might be helpful. At the end of the book you will find a Browse and Learn More section, a glossary, and an index. The Browse and Learn More section lists general publishing books and websites to explore. The glossary gives brief definitions of words that relate to education, career training, or employment that you may be unfamiliar with. The index includes all the job titles mentioned in the book.

It is not too soon to think about your future. We hope you discover several possible career choices in the publishing industry. Happy hunting!

Advertising and Marketing Workers

What Advertising and Marketing Workers Do

Advertising workers sell space for ads in newspapers and magazines. They also may sell ads on the Internet or airtime for commercials on radio and television. These sales workers are also called *advertising sales executives.* Advertising workers call or visit companies or advertising agencies that might want to develop commercials or run ads. The sales worker and the client discuss the different lengths or sizes of advertisements available and their costs. In magazines and newspapers, for example, ad space may be sold by the inch, the number of words, the fraction of a page, or the full page.

Marketing workers collect and analyze all kinds of information to develop marketing campaigns. These campaigns help newspaper, book, periodical, and other types of companies sell their products. Marketing workers also develop a distribution plan for products. If a product is expected to sell well to a certain group, for example, marketing professionals must decide how to deliver to members of that group based on when and where they shop. Along with the public relations department, marketing workers contact members of the press, such as book reviewers, to deliver product information to the public. Additionally, marketing workers called *media buyers* contact newspapers,

> **Did You Know?**
>
> Employment in the advertising industry is predicted to increase by 19 percent through 2012, according to the *Career Guide to Industries.*

> **Advertising and Marketing Magazines on the Web**
>
> **Advertising Age**
> http://www.adage.com
>
> **ADWEEK**
> http://www.adweek.com/aw/index.jsp
>
> **Mediaweek**
> http://www.mediaweek.com/mediaweek/index.jsp

magazines, and radio and television stations to buy time to advertise their product. They ensure that the ads appear when and where they should and negotiate costs for ad placement.

Whether they are trying to sell advertising space or determine the best way to market a new book or specialty newspaper, advertising and marketing workers need to know what kinds of people read their publications. They try to learn everything they can about their audiences, including information such as age, sex, income, and shopping habits. Advertising workers use this research when they approach the companies that want to advertise their products to specific groups of people. Marketing workers use this information to determine how they will market each product.

The work environment for advertising and marketing employees can range from the simple offices at a small newspaper to the glamorous production studios at a national television station. Although work in this field can be fast-paced and stressful, it can also be exciting and rewarding.

A team of advertising workers discusses an upcoming advertising campaign. (Photodisc)

Advertising and Marketing Glossaries on the Web

Glossary of Terms Used in Advertising and Marketing Communications
http://www.garyeverhart.com/glossary_of_advertising_terms.htm

The University of Texas at Austin: Department of Advertising
http://advertising.utexas.edu/research/terms

Advertising and marketing managers plan, organize, direct, and coordinate advertising and marketing campaigns. They may oversee an entire company, a geographical territory of a company's operations, or a specific department within a company.

Education and Training

If you want to be an advertising or marketing worker, you must have at least a high school education. Many employers also require a bachelor's degree. Useful courses to take in both the high school and college are communications, business, economics, advertising, marketing, English, psychology, and speech. People with sales experience have a better chance of getting hired as sales workers. Previous work experience at a radio station, television station, newspaper, or magazine is also helpful. For specialized publications, such as those focusing on electronics, health, or law, for example, it is helpful to have knowledge in that particular field before selling ad space to specialists. With the growing trend of

EXPLORING

- In your local community, volunteer or work part time at a local newspaper or magazine.
- Craft fairs, holiday boutiques, and rummage sales may provide you with opportunities to create and place ads and work with the local media to get exposure for the events.
- Ask your teacher to set up an information interview with an advertising or marketing worker.

FOR MORE INFO

For information on student chapters, contact
American Advertising Federation
1101 Vermont Avenue, NW, Suite 500
Washington, DC 20005-6306
Tel: 202-898-0089
Email: aaf@aaf.org
http://www.aaf.org

For profiles of advertising workers and career information, contact
Advertising Educational Foundation
220 East 42nd Street, Suite 3300
New York, NY 10017-5806
Tel: 212-986-8060
http://www.aded.org

For career information, contact
American Marketing Association
311 South Wacker Drive, Suite 5800
Chicago, IL 60606
Tel: 800-262-1150
Email: info@ama.org
http://www.marketingpower.com

advertising on the Internet, you should become familiar with computers and the Web.

Earnings

According to a survey by the National Association of Colleges and Employers, advertising majors entering the job market in 2003 had average starting salaries of $29,495, while marketing majors averaged $34,038. According to the U.S. Department of Labor, advertising managers had median annual salaries of $57,130 in 2002, and marketing managers earned median salaries of $78,250.

Outlook

Employment for advertising and marketing workers is expected to grow faster than the average over the next decade. There will be many applicants for each job opening, however, so those with more experience and skill will have an advantage. Starting in a small town or at a small publication can provide workers with valuable experience to move on to larger markets such as Chicago, Los Angeles, and New York.

Although newspaper sales are in decline, there is growth in special-interest publications. The Internet is providing advertising activity all around the world. The Web promises advertisers exposure in 65 million American households. All of this advertising activity will increase opportunities for advertising and marketing workers.

Art Directors

What Art Directors Do

Art directors are in charge of all images that appear in print (newspapers, books, magazines, and advertisements) and on screen (television, movies, videos, and the Web). Art directors work at advertising agencies, film studios, publishing companies, theater companies, and other organizations that produce or use visual elements, such as photography, illustrations, props, costumes, and sets. Art directors hire illustrators, photographers, animators, set and costume designers, and models and find existing illustrations and photos. Sometimes they combine new and existing art to create the desired visual effect.

Some art directors work with printed material, such as newspapers, magazines, and books. They are experts in arranging the text, pictures, and other visual elements, and in using color, photography, and different kinds of lettering called typefaces.

In print media, art directors sketch a design of what the page will look like. They block out areas for text, artwork, and other graphics. The art director then selects illustrators, photographers, or graphic designers to create the finished art for the project. A production editor or graphic designer puts the finished pieces together into a final form, usually a computer layout file. The art director sees every part of the process and gives approval or orders changes. Once the art director is satisfied with the final proof, the project is ready to be printed.

Did You Know?

There are nearly 2,400 art directors employed in the newspaper, book, and directory publishing industries, according to the U.S. Department of Labor.

Technology plays an important role in the art director's job. Most art directors, for example, use a variety of computer software programs, including Adobe InDesign, PageMaker, FrameMaker, Illustrator, Photoshop, QuarkXPress, and CorelDRAW. Many others create and oversee websites for clients and work with other interactive media and materials, including CD-ROM, touch-screens, multidimensional visuals, and new animation programs.

EXPLORING

- Join a free online art club, such as Paleta: The Art Project (http://www.paletaworld.org).
- Work on the staff of your school newspaper, magazine, or yearbook.
- Develop your own artistic talent by reading books and practicing drawing skills or taking art classes.
- Visit art galleries and museums. Study paintings, as well as magazines, motion pictures, product packaging, videos, or commercials. Notice color, composition, balance, mood, and other visual elements.
- Get a part-time job in the art department of a local newspaper or advertising agency.

Education and Training

To prepare for a career as an art director, concentrate on art and computer classes, as well as math. Most art directors have at least a bachelor's degree, usually in graphic design or fine art. A few go on to earn master's degrees. Film art directors can earn a degree in film, directing, animation, or cinematography.

Art directors rarely start out as art directors. Their first jobs may be as graphic designers, production assistants, or illustrators. As they gain experience and learn the ins and outs of the print or film industries, they move into higher positions until they become art directors.

Earnings

In 2002 art directors employed in the publishing industry had mean annual salaries of $65,280, according to the U.S. Department of Labor. Salaries for art directors employed in all

To Be a Successful Art Director, You Should . . .

- be creative and imaginative
- have knowledge of computer hardware and software
- work well with all types of people
- be able to handle the stress of constant deadlines
- have excellent time management skills
- stay up to date with current technology

industries ranged from less than $32,410 to more than $115,570.

Outlook

Overall employment in the publishing industry is expected to decline over the next decade, but there will always be a need

FOR MORE INFO

For more information on the advertising industry, contact
American Advertising Federation
1101 Vermont Avenue, NW, Suite 500
Washington, DC 20005-6306
Tel: 202-898-0089
Email: aaf@aaf.org
http://www.aaf.org

For more information on graphic design, contact
American Institute of Graphic Arts
164 Fifth Avenue
New York, NY 10010
Tel: 212-807-1990
Email: comments@aiga.org
http://www.aiga.org

For information on workshops for high school students, contact
Art Directors Club
106 West 29th Street
New York, NY 10001
Tel: 212-643-1440
Email: info@adcglobal.org
http://www.adcglobal.org

for talented art directors to oversee the design of books and other publications. Competition for these jobs will be stiff, though. It takes many years assisting in design and layout before you can become a director.

One area that shows particularly good promise for growth is the retail industry, since more and more large retail establishments—especially catalog houses—will be employing in-house advertising art directors.

Bindery Workers

What Bindery Workers Do

Binding, or finishing, is the final step in the printing process. *Bindery workers* take the printed pages that go into books, magazines, pamphlets, catalogs, and other materials and fold, cut, sew, staple, stitch, and/or glue them together to produce the finished product. Bindery workers typically work in commercial printing plants or specialized bindery shops.

The average bindery worker today is a skilled machine operator. Collating, inserting, and other bindery tasks are sometimes done by hand, but the bulk of binding processes are automated: cutting, folding, gathering, stitching, gluing, trimming, and wrapping. Finishing also might include embossing, die cutting, and foil stamping.

Bindery work ranges from simple to complex. Some binding jobs, such as preparing leaflets or newspaper inserts, require only a single step—in this case folding. The most complicated binding work is edition binding, or the production of books from large printed sheets of paper. Book pages are usually not produced individually but are printed on a large sheet of paper, six or eight at a time. These large sheets are folded by a machine into units called *signatures*, and the signatures are joined together in the proper order to make a complete book. The signatures are then assembled by a gathering

---

To Be a Successful Bindery Worker, You Should . . .

- be attentive to detail
- have good eyesight
- have finger dexterity to count, insert, paste, and fold materials
- be a good communicator
- have strong mathematical and mechanical aptitude

machine and sewed or glued together to make what is called a *book block*. The book blocks are compressed in a machine to ensure compactness and uniform thickness, trimmed to the proper size, and reinforced with fabric strips that are glued along the spine. The covers for the book are created separately and are pasted or glued to the book block by a machine. Books may undergo a variety of finishing operations, such as gilding the edges of pages or wrapping with dust jackets, before they are inspected and packed for shipment. A similar procedure is used in the binding of magazines, catalogs, and directories.

In large binderies, the operations are usually done in an assembly-line fashion by workers who are trained in just one or two procedures. For example, a *stitcher operator* runs the machines that stitch printed matter along its spine or edge. Other workers might specialize in the cutting, folding, or gathering processes. Much of this work involves setting up equipment and adjusting it as needed during the binding process.

Bindery workers assemble books in a printing plant. (Photodisc)

Education and Training

High school students can gain some exposure to bindery work by taking shop courses or attending a vocational-technical high school.

Most bindery workers train for this field on the job. Formal apprenticeships are becoming less common but are available for workers interested in acquiring highly specialized skills. Postsecondary training in graphic arts, often offered at community and junior colleges, is also useful.

Shorter apprenticeship programs combining on-the-job training with classroom instruction may be required for union shops. Four-year college programs in graphic arts are recommended for people who want to work in bindery shop management. With today's fast-changing technology, all bindery workers are likely to need occasional retraining once employed in a job.

EXPLORING
- Take a tour of a bindery in your area.
- Obtain a summer job in a local bindery, where you can observe operations and talk with experienced employees.
- Ask your teacher to set up an information interview with a bindery worker.

Types of Binderies

edition binderies specialize in large volumes of books and magazines

pamphlet binderies specialize in making pamphlets

trade or job binderies binderies that finish smaller quantities on a contract basis for printers and publishers

manifold or loose-leaf binderies specialize in binding blank pages and forms into ledgers, notebooks, checkbooks, calendars, and notepads

hand book binderies small shops that bind special-edition books or restore and rebind old books

FOR MORE INFO

For information on education and training programs available through local union schools, contact
Graphic Communications International Union
1900 L Street, NW
Washington, DC 20036
Tel: 202-462-1400
http://www.gciu.org

For information on the career of bindery worker, visit the GAIN website.
GAIN: Graphic Arts Information Network
http://www.gain.net/PIA_GATF/learning_center/binding.html

For comprehensive educational and career information about the graphic communications industry, visit
Graphic Comm Central
http://teched.vt.edu/gcc

Earnings

Bindery workers had median salaries of $21,861 in 2002, according to the U.S. Department of Labor. The lowest paid 10 percent earned $14,456 or less, while the highest paid 10 percent earned $37,336 or more.

Workers that belong to a union usually have higher earnings. The average workweek for bindery workers is between 35 and 40 hours, although many work more than that. Generally, full-time employees are paid overtime wages if they work more than 40 hours. Benefits typically include health insurance, paid vacation time, and retirement plans.

Outlook

Employment for bindery workers will decline over the next decade. Because the binding process is becoming increasingly mechanized, the need for workers to do certain tasks is dwindling. New, automated equipment in binderies can perform a number of operations in sequence, beginning with raw stock at one end of the process and finishing with the final product. These machines shorten production time, increase plant productivity, and reduce overall labor requirements.

Knowledgeable workers, however, are needed to oversee the use of new technologies. Bindery workers with up-to-date computer skills and mechanical aptitude will have the best opportunities in the field. Most full-time job opportunities will come from the need to replace workers who leave the field for different jobs, retirement, or other reasons.

Book Editors

What Book Editors Do

Book editors prepare written material for publication. In small publishing companies, the same editor may guide the material through all the stages of the publishing process. They work with typesetters, printers, designers, advertising agencies, and other members of the publishing industry. In larger companies, editors may be more specialized and take care of only a part of the publishing process.

Acquisitions editors locate new writers and new projects. They find new ideas for books that will sell well. They find writers who can create the books. Sometimes they assign a series of books to one author. Acquisitions editors make sure authors turn in their manuscripts on time. They usually work with several authors at a time.

Content editors take the manuscript written by an author and polish the work into a finished book. They correct grammar, spelling, and style, and check all the facts. They make sure the book reads well and suggest changes to the author if it does not.

Copy editors help content editors polish the author's writing. They review each page and make all the changes required to give the book a good writing style.

Line editors review the text to make sure specific style rules are obeyed. They make sure the same spelling is

Parts of a Book

- Cover
- Front matter
  - Title page
  - Copyright page
  - Table of contents
  - Preface
  - Introduction
- Text
- Back matter
  - Notes
  - Appendix
  - Glossary
  - Bibliography
  - Index

18 Discovering Careers for Your Future: Publishing

Book editors must have an excellent eye for detail and be able to work under tight deadlines. (Photodisc)

What Proofreaders Do

Proofreaders carefully read text before it is printed. They use special symbols and abbreviations to mark the text. They look for errors in:

○ Spelling: Are all the words spelled correctly and consistently? For example, if a writer uses "on-line" in one sentence and "online" in another sentence, the proofreader makes sure the same spelling is used throughout the book.

○ Grammar: The proofreader checks for things like subject-verb agreement, run-on sentences, sentence fragments, awkward phrases, and other problems in sentence construction.

○ Punctuation: Proofreaders check for correct use of commas, colons, semicolons, periods, quotation marks, apostrophes, dashes, and parentheses.

○ Sense: Sometimes sentences or paragraphs are printed out of order, or sometimes words get left out. The proofreader marks text that doesn't seem to make sense.

○ Style: Proofreaders check for correct *italic* or **boldface** type. They look at headings, text, and page numbers to make sure they are in the correct typeface, column width, and position.

used for words where more than one spelling is correct (for example, grey and gray).

Fact checkers and *proofreaders* read the manuscript to make sure everything is spelled correctly and that all the facts in the text have been checked. They may check by calling experts, or the people quoted, or they may look in other publications to see if the information has been printed before.

Production editors work with artists to get the cover and pages designed. They work with illustrators and photographers to create artwork for the book. They manage the page layout process. They make sure all the parts of the book get to the printer on time. At large publishing companies, these duties are often handled by an art director.

Most editors work a 35-to-40-hour week. But all editors work with schedules and deadlines, so they sometimes have to work overtime to get a publication out on time. Most editors work in clean, quiet offices. Others may work in noisy, crowded rooms where telephones are ringing and people are typing.

EXPLORING

- Become a student member of the American Copy Editors Society (http://www.copydesk.org).
- Take an editing test at http://www.copydesk.org/guidelines.htm to gauge your skills.
- Write something every day. You may come up with an idea for a story, essay, or poem. When you have written a piece, go back and rework your writing until it is as good as you can make it.
- Ask your teacher to set up an information interview with a book, newspaper, or magazine editor.
- One of the best ways to explore the field of editing is to work on a school newspaper or yearbook. Try writing, reporting, proofreading, desktop publishing, printing, or any other task related to publishing. This will help you to understand the editing and publishing process.
- Publish your own book or newsletter using your home computer.

Education and Training

If you want to be a book editor, you should take English, social studies, and computer classes. In high school, you should also study English literature, foreign languages, history, and computers. For most editorial jobs you need to know computer word-processing programs.

FOR MORE INFO

For comprehensive information on copyediting careers, including editing tests, quizzes, discussion groups, and career guidance, visit the ACES website.
American Copy Editors Society (ACES)
3 Healy Street
Huntington, NY 11743
http://www.copydesk.org

For general information about publishing, contact
Association of American Publishers
71 Fifth Avenue
New York, NY 10003
Tel: 212-255-0200
http://www.publishers.org

For information on the types of publishing, a glossary of publishing terms, profiles of companies, and a detailed breakdown of departments in a publishing company, visit
Bookjobs.com
http://www.bookjobs.com

You will need a college education for an editorial job. Many employers prefer to hire people who have a degree in English, journalism, communication arts, history, philosophy, or social sciences. Some colleges offer special courses in book publishing or editing.

Earnings

Experienced editors earned yearly salaries that ranged from less than $24,010 to more than $76,620 in 2002, according to the U.S. Department of Labor. The median annual salary for editors employed by newspaper, periodical, book, and directory publishers was $40,280 in 2002.

Outlook

Employment for editors will grow about as fast as the average for all other occupations over the next decade. A number of factors account for this positive outlook. Demand is growing for books, magazines, and other periodicals, and many businesses and nonprofit organizations are developing newsletters and other publications. The growth of the Internet has also created demand for editors with experience in this medium. Despite these positive developments, the competition for editing jobs will be even stiffer than it has been in the past. Editors who specialize in a specific subject, such as medicine, law, business, or science, will enjoy the best opportunities in the coming years.

Columnists

What Columnists Do

Columnists write their opinions for newspapers, magazines, and websites. Some columnists write about personal experience. Others write about current events.

Columns are written on a schedule, perhaps every day, week, or month, depending on how often the newspaper or magazine comes out. Like other journalists, columnists must complete their work by strict deadlines.

Columnists sometimes specialize in one area. Some may write humor columns, while others write in a more serious tone about government and politics, health, or business.

Columnists search through newspapers, magazines, and the Internet for ideas. Coming up with new ideas is one of the hardest parts of being a columnist. Next, they do research to gather facts to support their viewpoints. Finally, they write their columns, usually on a computer.

Most columnists work in newsrooms or magazine offices. But some work out of their homes or private offices.

Some columnists become famous after their columns run in newspapers across the country. For example, the late Mike Royko started writing his column in Chicago, but his work was published in newspapers around the

Famous Columnists

Molly Ivins (politics)
George F. Will (politics)
Ann Landers (personal advice)
Abigail Van Buren (aka Dear Abby) (personal advice)
Dave Barry (humor)
Garrison Keillor (humor)
Tony Kornheiser (humor/sports)
Jerome Holtzman (sports)
Peter Gammons (sports)

EXPLORING

- A good way to explore this career is to work for your school newspaper and perhaps write your own column.
- Participation in debate clubs will help you form opinions and express them clearly.
- Read your local newspaper. Find a story that interests you. What do you think about the topic? Do you agree or disagree with the writer? Write your own opinions.

country, making him a familiar name to readers in many cities and towns.

Most columnists start out as reporters. After they gain experience, they may be offered a columnist's job.

Columns are different than regular news stories because they usually take a side on an issue. A columnist must have strong opinions. They must clearly explain facts and observations that support their opinions. They must not be afraid when people disagree or challenge their ideas.

Almost every newspaper runs some type of column. Newspapers employ their own columnists or publish columns they buy from syndicates (companies that sell published material to several newspapers at once) or both.

Education and Training

Reading and writing are important subjects for future columnists. In high school, you should take English, journalism, social studies, speech, computer science, and typing. It is a good idea to try to write for your school newspaper or yearbook.

After high school, you must go to a university and earn at least a bachelor's degree. Most editors prefer that their employees hold a degree in journalism. Others prefer applicants with a bachelor's degree in liberal arts and a master's degree in journalism.

Much of your training will come on the job as a reporter. Reporters learn the key parts of being a columnist: interviewing, research, and people skills. Also, reporters learn how to

> ## Profile: Art Buchwald
>
> Art Buchwald, born in 1925, is a U.S. journalist who became famous for his political columns. He won a Pulitzer Prize in 1982 for his commentary about political figures.
>
> Buchwald was born in Mount Vernon, New York. He attended the University of Southern California from 1945 to 1948. Then he went to Paris, where he began to write a humorous column on life in Europe. He moved to Washington, D.C., in 1962.
>
> *Laid Back in Washington* (1982) is a collection of his newspaper columns. *Leaving Home: A Memoir* was published in 1994. His other books include *Art Buchwald's Paris* (1954), *I Chose Capitol Punishment* (1963), *I Never Danced at the White House* (1973), *I'll Always Have Paris* (1997), and *We'll Laugh Again* (2003).

manage their time, write quickly and to the point, and finish before deadline.

Earnings

Columnists' salaries depend on many factors, such as newspaper or magazine size and location, and how often the column is published. Columnists usually make higher salaries than reporters. Columnists who were employed by newspapers and magazine publishers had median annual earnings of $29,000 in 2002, according to the U.S. Department of Labor. Experienced columnists can earn top salaries of $70,000 or more.

Outlook

Employment of columnists is expected to stay about the same in coming years. Newspaper jobs will decrease, but magazine writing jobs could increase. The growth of online media outlets will provide columnists with more employment opportunities. There will be strong competition for jobs in this career. The best place to start is at smaller publications, where newspaper reporters and magazine editorial assistants take on many tasks, but where they also are promoted faster. However, bigger publications may offer bigger paychecks.

FOR MORE INFO

For information on careers in nonfiction writing, contact
American Society of Journalists and Authors
1501 Broadway, Suite 302
New York, NY 10036
Tel: 212-997-0947
http://www.asja.org

For general educational information on all areas of journalism (newspapers, magazines, television, radio, and the Internet), contact
Association for Education in Journalism and Mass Communication
234 Outlet Pointe Boulevard
Columbia, SC 29210-5667
Tel: 803-798-0271
http://www.aejmc.org

For information on careers in the newspaper industry, contact
Dow Jones Newspaper Fund
PO Box 300
Princeton, NJ 08543-0300
Email: newsfund@wsj.dowjones.com
http://djnewspaperfund.dowjones.com

For information on journalism careers, contact
Society of Professional Journalists
3909 North Meridian Street
Indianapolis, IN 46208
Tel: 317-927-8000
Email: questions@spj.org
http://www.spj.org

Visit the following website for comprehensive information on journalism careers, summer programs, and college journalism programs.
High School Journalism
http://www.highschooljournalism.org

Desktop Publishing Specialists

What Desktop Publishing Specialists Do

If you have made flyers to advertise a music recital or printed up programs for a school play, then you have probably worked with computers, desktop publishing software, and printers. *Desktop publishing specialists* do this for a living. They create reports, brochures, books, business cards, and other documents. They work with files others have created, or they compose original text and graphics for their clients or employers. Desktop publishing specialists have graphic design skills, proofreading skills, and a knowledge of illustration and page layout software. They also have sales and marketing abilities.

Individuals and small business owners hire desktop publishing specialists to create printed documents and Internet Web pages. Programs such as FreeHand, Illustrator, Photo-Shop, QuarkXpress, InDesign, and

> **Words to Learn**
>
> **bleed** an element that extends to the edge of a page
> **body copy** the main text in a publication
> **copyfitting** forcing text to fit a space by editing copy, changing the spacing between letters or lines of type, or adjusting type size
> **flip** to change an item so that it appears as a mirror image of the original
> **leading** the space between lines of text
> **pica** a measurement used in printing; there are 6 picas in 1 inch
> **point** a unit of typographic measurement; 1 point is 1/72 of an inch, and there are 12 points in 1 pica
> **registration** the alignment of overlaying pieces
> **resolution** sharpness of detail; usually measured in dots per inch

EXPLORING

- Work on your school paper and yearbook to get experience with page layout, typesetting, word processing, and how to meet deadlines.
- Experiment with your home computer or a computer at school or the library. Play around with various graphic design and page layout programs.
- If you subscribe to an Internet service, take advantage of any free Web space available to you and design your own home page.
- Join computer clubs and volunteer at small organizations to produce newsletters and flyers.

PageMaker are popular desktop publishing programs. Desktop publishing specialists create interesting graphics, arrange the text on the page, select font types and sizes, arrange column widths, and check for proper spacing between letters, words, and columns. Proofreading is also important: desktop publishing specialists check for spelling and typing errors. They prepare documents for printing, so they also handle issues such as resolution for graphics and photos, pagination, registration, and color specification.

Desktop publishing specialists work closely with their clients, making sure to create the documents according to specifications. After creating the file and getting final approval from clients, they either give the files on disk to the customer or, in some cases, they give files to the printer and manage the project through the printing process.

Education and Training

Desktop publishing specialists need a good eye for detail and excellent computer and artistic skills. In high school, take computer classes that teach both hardware and software. Photography classes can teach you about color, composition, and design. Art classes will help you learn graphic design skills, while English classes help you learn about editing and composition.

A college degree is not required to become a desktop publishing specialist, but it may be helpful to earn a two-year associate's degree in graphic design, commercial art, or advertising.

Earnings

Wages for desktop publishing specialists vary depending on experience, training, region in which they work, and size of the company. Entry-level desktop publishing specialists with little or no experience generally earn minimum wage. The U.S. Department of Labor reports that desktop publishing specialists employed in all industries had median annual earnings that ranged from less than $18,670 to more than $52,540 in 2002. Desktop publishing specialists who were employed in the newspaper, book, periodical publishing industries had median annual earnings of $28,050 in 2002.

Read All about it

Kursmark, Louise M. *How to Start a Home-Based Desktop Publishing Business.* 3rd ed. Guilford, Conn.: Globe Pequot Press, 2002.

Parker, Roger C. *Looking Good in Print.* 5th ed. Phoenix, Ariz.: Paraglyph Press, 2003.

Weixel, Suzanne. *Desktop Publishing BASICS.* Boston: Course Technology, 2003.

Williams, Robin. *The Non-Designer's Design Book.* 2nd ed. Berkeley, Calif.: Peachpit Press, 2003.

Williams, Robin, and John Tollett. *Robin Williams Design Workshop.* Berkeley, Calif.: Peachpit Press, 2000.

Outlook

Employment of desktop publishing specialists will grow faster than the average over the next decade. Desktop publishing is rapidly replacing compositing and typesetting as a cost-effective means of book and periodical production. Commercial printing and publishing companies are expected to provide the most new positions for workers in this field.

FOR MORE INFO

For career information, contact
Graphic Arts Education and Research Foundation
1899 Preston White Drive
Reston, VA 20191
Tel: 703-264-7200
Email: gaerf@npes.org
http://www.gaerf.org

To read A Career in Technical Communication, What's In It For You?, *visit the STC website.*
Society for Technical Communication (STC)
901 North Stuart Street, Suite 904
Arlington, VA 22203
Email: stc@stc.org
http://www.stc.org/PDF_Files/aCareer.pdf

To subscribe to DesktopPublishers World Update, *a free email newsletter, visit*
DesktopPublishers.com
http://www.dtpjournal.com

For comprehensive educational and career information about the graphic communications industry, visit
Graphic Comm Central
http://teched.vt.edu/gcc

Graphic Designers

What Graphic Designers Do

Graphic designers design a wide variety of materials including advertisements, displays, packaging, signs, computer graphics and games, book and magazine covers and interiors, animated characters, websites, and company logos for their clients.

Graphic designers receive materials for their assignments from editors and writers, illustrators, and photographers. They might receive special instructions from art directors or publishers. They have to consider the medium—print, computer, or film—and the audience. They decide on a central point of focus, such as the title of a magazine article or the name of a product on a package. They size the lettering; choose and size the artwork, whether it's an illustration, photograph, or logo; and choose colors. Staff designers for magazines, newspapers, and other periodicals usually have to follow a regular format that makes every issue look consistent. Some graphic designers create logos for companies or draw charts and graphs.

Graphic design is a process. For example, when designing a cover for a book, designers make two or three rough designs for the client to look at. The client might choose one of the designs immediately, or ask a designer to change the type size, color, or another element. Designers rework their pieces until their clients are satisfied. Then they prepare the final design.

Type Choices

lower case	***bold italic***
UPPER CASE	SMALL CAPS
roman	underline
bold	shadow
italic	outline

EXPLORING

- Take art and design courses at your school or at community centers or art schools.
- Learn different software programs for page layout and illustration.
- Participate in building sets for plays, setting up exhibits, planning seasonal and holiday displays, and preparing concert programs and other printed materials.
- Work on the layout of your school newspaper or yearbook.

Each medium is different. Graphic designers in film and television design the credits and other type that appears on screen. They also work on animated graphics, maps, and charts. In product packaging, designers must be able to visualize a three-dimensional object that will be printed from a flat piece of artwork. Websites require a different arrangement of type and pictures than magazine pages. Graphic designers usually specialize in one of these media.

Graphic designers are employed by publishing companies, printers, design studios, advertising firms, television studios, manufacturing firms, and retail stores. Many designers work independently as freelancers. All designers today do their work on computers, using illustration, photo manipulation, scanning, and page-layout software.

Education and Training

High school classes in mathematics, art, and computer science are a good foundation for this field. Most employers prefer to hire people who have had formal art education. The best preparation after high school is a four-year art school program that leads to a bachelor of fine arts degree. There are art schools that offer a specialty in graphic design or advertising design. Some graphic designers receive their training at vocational schools that teach the required technical skills for a beginning job. Since computer skills are increasingly important, some formal education in computer graphics is highly recommended.

Designers often start out as production artists or computer graphic technicians. Some even work as art teachers before becoming full-time designers.

Earnings

Graphic designers earned salaries that ranged from less than $21,860 to $64,160 or more in 2002, according to the U.S. Department of Labor. Graphic designers employed in the newspaper, periodical, and book industries had median annual earnings of $31,670 in 2002. Salaried designers who advance to the

How Freelancers Find Clients

Many graphic designers work as freelancers. This means they are self-employed and seek their own assignments. It can be difficult, especially when starting out, to find new clients who will hire them. Freelancers have to spend a lot of time marketing their talents and finding assignments. Here are some methods they use.

- Friends may have contacts in different businesses. They might be able to arrange an interview with a potential client.
- Professional organizations hold meetings and advertise available jobs for their members.
- Demonstrations and classes can offer opportunities to meet other designers and clients.
- Freelancers sometimes design and print a brochure that demonstrates their talent and then send it to potential clients.
- Freelancers can also make contacts by attending meetings, lectures, or gatherings for causes that interest them. For example, a graphic designer might attend a food-related convention and meet a restaurant owner who needs menu designs.

position of design manager or design director earn about $60,000 a year. The owner of a consulting firm can make $85,000 or more.

Outlook

Graphic designers should have very good employment prospects over the next several years. As computer graphics and Web-based technology continue to advance, there will be a need for well-trained graphic designers. Companies for which graphic design was once too time-consuming or costly are now sprucing up company newsletters and magazines, among other things. This requires the skills of design professionals. Competition for jobs in graphic design is expected to be strong. Beginners and designers with only average talent or without formal education and skills may have difficulty finding jobs.

FOR MORE INFO

For more information about careers in graphic design and a list of college programs, visit the AIGA website.
American Institute of Graphic Arts (AIGA)
164 Fifth Avenue
New York, NY 10010
Tel: 212-807-1990
Email: comments@aiga.org
http://www.aiga.org

For a list of accredited college art and design programs, contact
National Association of Schools of Art and Design
11250 Roger Bacon Drive, Suite 21
Reston, VA 20190-5248
Tel: 703-437-0700
Email: info@arts-accredit.org
http://nasad.arts-accredit.org

For information about publication design, contact
Society of Publication Designers
60 East 42nd Street, Suite 721
New York, NY 10165
Tel: 212-983-8585
Email: mail@spd.org
http://www.spd.org

Illustrators

What Illustrators Do

Illustrators create artwork with a variety of media—pencil, pen and ink, pastels, paints (oil, acrylic, watercolor), airbrush, collage, and computer programs. Illustrations are used to decorate, describe, inform, instruct, and draw attention. Illustrations appear in books, magazines, newspapers, signs and billboards, packaging (everything from milk cartons to DVDs), websites, computer programs, greeting cards, calendars, stationery, and direct mail.

Illustrators often work as part of a creative team that includes graphic designers, photographers, and calligraphers (those who draw lettering). Most illustrators are self-employed, but some work in advertising agencies, design firms, commercial art firms, or printing and publishing companies. They are also employed in the motion picture and television industries, retail stores, catalog companies, and public relations firms.

Some illustrators specialize. *Medical illustrators*, for example, make drawings, paintings, and three-dimensional models of medical procedures and specimens. Their work appears in textbooks, advertisements, medical journals, videotapes, and films. It may

Read All about It

Edwards, Betty. *The New Drawing on the Right Side of the Brain.* New York: J. P. Tarcher, 1999.

Hammond, Lee. *Draw Fashion Models! Discover Drawing Series.* Cincinnati, Ohio: North Light Books, 1998.

Hodges, Elaine R. S., ed. *The Guild Handbook of Scientific Illustration.* 2nd ed. Hoboken, N.J.: John Wiley & Sons, 2003.

Ireland, Patrick John. *Figure Templates for Fashion Illustration: Over 150 Templates for Fashion Design.* London, U.K.: Batsford, 2003.

West, Keith R. *How to Draw Plants: The Techniques of Botanical Illustration.* Portland, Oreg.: Timber Press, 1996.

EXPLORING

- Take art classes that allow you to experiment with different media.
- Keep a sketch diary in which you draw every day.
- Submit artwork for your school newspaper, yearbook, or literary publication.
- Join an art club at your school or community center.
- Make posters for school and community events.

also be used at medical conventions, in public exhibits, and as teaching aids in classrooms and laboratories.

Fashion illustrators work for advertising agencies, newspapers, catalog houses, and fashion magazines. They attend fashion shows and work closely with fashion designers to make sure clothing colors and styles are represented accurately.

Natural science illustrators create illustrations of plants and wildlife. They often work at museums such as the Smithsonian Institution.

Most illustrators become known for their particular style and medium (paint, pen and ink, pastel, pencil, and collage to name a few). Until they become well known, illustrators spend a great deal of time showing their portfolio to clients.

Education and Training

To become an illustrator, you must develop your artistic and creative abilities. Take art classes and learn computer illustration programs as well.

Talent is perhaps more important to an illustrator's success than education or training. Education, however, will teach you about new techniques and media and help you build your portfolio. Whether you plan to look for full-time employment or freelance assignments, you will need a portfolio that contains samples of your best work. Employers are especially interested in work that has been published

An illustrator creates artwork for a new publication. (Corbis)

> ### Profile: Maxfield Parrish (1870–1966)
>
> Maxfield Parrish was an American illustrator and painter known for his use of color and for his decorative, humorous pictures.
>
> Parrish was born in Philadelphia and attended Haverford College and the Pennsylvania Academy of Fine Arts. He also studied with the illustrator Howard Pyle.
>
> Parrish illustrated Eugene Field's *Poems of Childhood,* Kenneth Grahame's *Golden Age,* and other books. He did advertisements, illustrations, and covers for such magazines as *Harper's Weekly.* Among his murals are Pied Piper in the Sheraton-Palace Hotel in San Francisco and Old King Cole in the St. Regis Hotel in New York City.

or printed. To find a salaried position as an illustrator, you will need at least a high school diploma and preferably an associate's degree in commercial art or fine art. Most medical illustrators have master's degrees from graduate programs in medical illustration. There are five of these programs in the United States, and each accepts only between three and 12 students each year.

Earnings

The pay for illustrations can be as little as a byline (a line under the title that gives your name). Using a byline during the beginning of your career may be worthwhile, so that many people can become familiar with your work. Experienced illustrators can earn several thousand dollars for a single work. Average earnings for full-time fine artists ranged from less than $16,900 to $73,560 or more a year in 2002, according to the U.S. Department of Labor. Fine artists employed by book, periodical, and directory publishers had median annual salaries of $61,100 in 2002. Medical illustrators earn salaries that range from $45,000 to $75,000 per year.

Outlook

Employment for artists is expected to grow about as fast as the average over the next several years. Employment will be even better for skilled illustrators as the print and electronic media and the film and video industries continue to expand.

The field of medical illustration is small, but the field of medicine and science in general is always growing, and medical illustrators will be needed to depict new techniques, procedures, and discoveries. There are few opportunities available in fashion illustration, since photography and film are more popular for magazines and catalogs.

FOR MORE INFO

For information on educational and career opportunities for medical illustrators, contact
Association of Medical Illustrators
5475 Mark Dabling Boulevard, Suite 108
Colorado Springs, CO 80918
Tel: 719-598-8622
Email: hq@ami.org
http://medical-illustrators.org

For information in union membership and links to portfolios of illustrators, visit the GAG website.
Graphic Artists Guild (GAG)
90 Johns Street, Suite 403
New York, NY 10038-3202
Tel: 212-791-3400
http://www.gag.org

This national institution offers exhibits, lectures, educational programs, and social exchange with other illustrators.

Society of Illustrators
128 East 63rd Street
New York, NY 10021-7303
Tel: 212-838-2560
http://www.societyillustrators.org

For information on membership, contact
Guild of Natural Science Illustrators
PO Box 652
Ben Franklin Station
Washington, DC 20044-0652
Tel: 301-309-1514
http://www.gnsi.org

For information on membership, contact
Society of Children's Book Writers and Illustrators
8271 Beverly Boulevard
Los Angeles, CA 90048
Tel: 323-782-1010
Email: scbwi@scbwi.org
http://www.scbwi.org

Indexers

What Indexers Do

An index is a list of words and phrases, usually organized alphabetically. It helps people find information in a book, magazine, or other publication. *Indexers* are the people who create indexes.

An index must include references to all the important information in a text. An indexer must be able to recognize this information and include it in the index under entry headings. Choosing helpful headings can be the most challenging part of an indexer's job. The best indexers start by asking themselves where the reader would look for certain information. Usually the indexer will include references under the key term from the text and under more general, but related, headings. References to George Washington, for instance, might be listed under Washington, George, but also under Presidents, Revolutionary War, and United States History.

There are several types of indexers. Some work with single volumes to compile back-of-book indexes. Your social studies textbook probably contains a good example of this sort of index. Other indexers create the indexes for multi-volume sets of books, such as an encyclopedia.

Can Computers Replace Human Indexers?

Computer programs can make it easier for indexers to edit, format, and sort text and handle page numbers. But computer programs can never completely replace people. Computers cannot understand or organize ideas and information in the text. For example, a book on astronomy might have a chapter about constellations and signs of the Zodiac but might never use the word *astrology*. Someone using the book, though, might look for this word in the index.

Source: American Society of Indexers

EXPLORING

○ Visit libraries and read indexes of all kinds.
○ Read basic books on indexing, such as *Indexing Books* (Chicago: University of Chicago Press, 1994), by Nancy Mulvany; *Indexing from A to Z* (New York: H.W. Wilson, 1991), by Hans Wellisch; or *Handbook of Indexing Techniques: A Guide for Beginning Indexers* (Aransas, Texas: Fetters InfoManagement Co., 2001), by Linda Fetters.
○ The American Society of Indexers publishes several helpful pamphlets on getting started in the indexing profession. (See For More Info.)

Because these indexes contain references to several volumes, they sometimes fill an entire volume themselves. Still other indexers develop the indexes for magazines and newspapers. These indexes are published at regular times throughout the year. They are extremely helpful to researchers who otherwise might have to search through every issue of a magazine to find a single reference.

Before personal computers were widely used, indexers did their work manually. They kept track of entry headings and page numbers on alphabetically arranged index cards. Some indexers still work this way, but today, there are many computer programs that make the indexer's job easier.

Some indexers are full-time employees at publishing companies. Others work as freelancers.

Education and Training

In high school, take English and computer science classes. History and other social science classes will familiarize you with a broad range of subjects that might be indexed. A bachelor's degree with a major in English or in library science usually is required for indexing positions. Indexers must be familiar with a wide variety of subjects in order to create detailed indexes, so a liberal arts background is recommended. Indexers must know how to use computers.

How It All Began

The first known finding list was compiled by Callimachus, a Greek poet and scholar from the 3rd century B.C. It provided a guide to the contents of the Alexandrian Library.

Primitive alphabetical indexes began to appear in the 16th century A.D. In 1614, the bishop of Petina, Antonio Zara, included an index in his *Anatomia ingeniorum et scientiarum* (*Anatomy of Talents and Sciences*). In 1677, Johann Jacob Hoffman added an index to his *Lexicon universale*. These early indexes were difficult to use because entries under each letter of the alphabet were not arranged alphabetically.

In the 18th century, alphabetic indexing improved. The index of Denis Diderot's (1713–84) *Encyclopedie,* for example, is alphabetized consistently throughout. In the 19th century, indexers began to make indexes that covered entire fields of knowledge. *The Reader's Guide to Periodic Literature,* published by H. W. Wilson Company of New York, is one of the best examples of an index that includes references to many publications.

Earnings

The average starting salary for indexers is $20,000 a year and, depending on their level of experience and the kind of projects they work on, they may earn up to $70,000 a year.

Outlook

As long as people continue to read and do research, they will need indexes and the people who create them. More publishers now use computer indexing programs, so the indexer will need knowledge of these programs. Since no computer program can replace a human being completely, however,

publishers of reference books, encyclopedias, and periodicals will continue to need people to make smart indexing decisions.

FOR MORE INFO

For comprehensive information about becoming an indexer, contact
American Society of Indexers
10200 West 44th Avenue, Suite 304
Wheat Ridge, CO 80033
Tel: 303-463-2887
Email: info@asindexing.org
http://www.asindexing.org

Literary Agents

What Literary Agents Do

Literary agents work for writers. They try to sell a writer's works to publishers and film and television producers. Clients of literary agents might include new or established authors, or actors, athletes, musicians, and other public figures who want to be authors. To give their clients more time to write and revise their work, agents sometimes manage writers' business affairs, including bookkeeping and preparing tax forms. Literary agents are also called *authors' agents* and *writers' representatives.*

Literary agents begin by reading and evaluating writers' manuscripts. Then they decide whether to represent those writers. Agents might suggest revisions to improve the manuscripts and make them more marketable. They contact editors, publishers, and producers and try to sell their clients' work to them. Editors and producers may also make certain suggestions about manuscripts, and the agent gives this information to the client.

After selling a client's manuscript, the literary agent negotiates a contract, working out pay rates and deadlines. They also may create publicity and schedule public appearances, depending on the nature of the written work and the author's popularity.

Literary agents must spend a great deal of time and effort on their work. They carefully read manuscripts. They establish and maintain good business relationships with publishers and producers. They study the literary

Starting Out

Many literary agents start out as journalists or editors. As they work with more and more authors during their careers, they become interested in representing them and selling authors' works to publishers.

Literary agents spend a considerable amount of time on the telephone with their clients and potential employers such as publishers. (Corbis)

and dramatic markets. Most literary agents often have to work evenings and weekends to meet with clients and potential buyers.

Most agents are based in Los Angeles or New York because of the many publishing companies and film and television studios in those cities. Experienced literary agents may travel around the country or even around the world to meet with clients and with buyers.

Education and Training

High school students who are interested in this type of career should take courses in literature, composition, drama, and business.

Words to Learn

advance the amount of money paid to an author before the book is published; authors usually receive one-half of this amount when they sign the contract and the other half when they turn in the final manuscript

boilerplate a standard contract; most authors and agents make many changes to the boilerplate before it is signed

copyright a means to protect an author's work; it recognizes the author as owner of the writing and gives the author the right to decide how the work will be used

royalties a percentage of the profits from the sale of a book paid to the author; for a standard hardcover book, an author usually receives 10 percent of the retail price on the first 5,000 copies sold, 12.5 percent of the retail price on the next 5,000 copies, and 15 percent after that

To Be a Successful Literary Agent, You Should . . .

- have a talent for recognizing and promoting talent
- have knowledge of the publishing industry and the editorial needs of each publisher
- be persistent
- be able to communicate easily with writers, editors, and other publishing industry professionals
- have strong negotiation skills

There are no formal or specific requirements for becoming a literary agent. A college degree, however, is a plus. In college, it is helpful to take classes in the liberal arts, performing arts, and business administration. Communications courses also will help you interact with clients and buyers.

Agents must know and understand the markets to which they are representing their clients, such as publishing and movie and television production companies and be able to judge which is the best market. They must know how to work with people in negotiating fair contracts. They must be sincere in promoting their clients' works.

Earnings

Those who begin their careers in an entry-level position with an agency might earn as much as an average office worker. At higher levels, earnings almost always are based on commission, which means that the agent

EXPLORING

- Learn about current trends in book publishing and the kinds of books that particular publishing houses issue.
- Read magazines such as *Publishers Weekly* (http://www.publishersweekly.com).
- Part-time or volunteer work at bookstores and libraries will help you become familiar with books and publishers.

will be paid a rate based on what the client earns. The standard rate is 4 percent to 20 percent of the client's earnings. Salaries range anywhere from $24,000 to $60,000, with a few making hundreds of thousands of dollars. Experienced literary agents with successful clients and good reputations earn the most money.

Outlook

Competition is very strong among literary agents. Many people who choose this profession do not succeed. Those who do succeed may be employed by a literary agency, working their way from an entry-level position to one of great responsibility. The very talented and hardworking eventually may become self-employed.

FOR MORE INFO

For information on the duties, responsibilities, and ethical expectations of agents, and for AAR's newsletter, contact or visit the AAR website.

Association of Authors' Representatives Inc. (AAR)
PO Box 237201
Ansonia Station
New York, NY 10003
Email: info@aar-online.org
http://www.aar-online.org

To read answers to frequently asked questions about agents and publishing, visit the following website:
Adler & Robin Books
http://www.adlerbooks.com/mostask.html

Magazine Editors

What Magazine Editors Do

The main duty of a *magazine editor* is to plan the contents of the magazine. The magazine editor assigns topics to writers and supervises the articles through publication. Some editors write editorials to mold and stimulate public opinion. Editors often write, but they more often rewrite or revise the work of others. Magazine editors have the authority to hire and fire writers. They also negotiate contracts and plan budgets.

At small magazines, a single editor may produce the entire magazine alone. At large publications, a *senior* or *executive editor* supervises the work of *associate editors* who are in charge of specific areas, such as sports, fashion, or politics. For example, a fashion magazine may have a beauty editor, features editor, short story editor, and fashion editor. Each editor is responsible for obtaining, proofing, rewriting, and sometimes writing

Questions Editors Ask

When editors read articles for the first time, they ask themselves questions like these:

- Is the topic well defined and focused?
- Does the article contain facts, arguments, and explanations? If there are opinions, are the opinions well supported?
- Are the facts and ideas organized in a logical order?
- Are the introduction and conclusion interesting and effective?
- Has the writer given all the facts and answered all the questions a reader might ask?
- Is the article interesting to read?
- Are words spelled correctly? Are the grammar and punctuation correct?

EXPLORING

- Keep a daily journal. Practice writing short stories, poetry, or essays. Rework your writing until it is as good as you can make it.
- Read all kinds of magazines and newspapers.
- Work on a school newspaper or other publication, such as literary magazine. Publish your classmates' work and hand out issues to students and parents.

articles. *Managing editors* coordinate copy flow and supervise production of pages for each issue. *Production editors* handle the layout of feature articles and art. They prepare the magazine for printing. Magazines also employ *researchers*, sometimes called *fact checkers*, to make sure the facts in an article are correct.

Magazine editors often have assistants in entry-level positions with titles such as *assistant editor* or *copy editor*. These assistants check manuscripts for grammar, punctuation, and spelling. They add or rearrange sentences to make the meaning clear, and they take out incorrect information. They also may write headlines or arrange the way a page is laid out in the magazine.

Magazine editors sometimes work in large and beautiful private offices and sometimes in cramped and noisy spaces that they share with others. The working conditions depend on the size and type of magazine. An editor's hours also depend on the type of magazine. Most editors work 35 to 40 hours a week. A weekly magazine has more deadlines than a quarterly magazine (one published only four times a year). Editors often work overtime to meet deadlines.

Education and Training

In high school, develop your writing, reading, and analytical skills by taking English and composition classes. Take history or politics classes to stay up to date with current and past events.

If your school offers journalism classes or, better yet, has a school newspaper, get involved. Any participation in the publishing process will be great experience, whether you are writing articles, proofreading copy, or laying out pages.

A college degree is required for a career as a magazine editor. Some employers look for a broad liberal arts background, but most prefer to hire people with degrees in communications, journalism, or English. Class work or a degree in the specific subject of a special-interest magazine—such as biology for a biology magazine—is also helpful.

Most magazine editors do not begin their careers as editors, but rise through the ranks. They work as editorial assistants, writers, or copy editors, then as assistant editors, before they become editors. It is helpful to have writing experience, because so much of an editor's job is supervising the work of writers.

Earnings

Salaries for editors ranged from $24,010 to $76,620 in 2002, according to the U.S. Department of Labor. Magazine editors

What Is a Stylebook?

Every publication must have rules, so that words and punctuation are consistent throughout the whole magazine. A stylebook is a book of rules for things like capitalization (Vice President or vice president?), abbreviations (Calif., Ill., and Wash. or CA, IL, and WA?), numbers (ten or 10?), punctuation (yes, no, and maybe or yes, no and maybe?), and hundreds of other questions and problems.

The most frequently used stylebooks are *The Chicago Manual of Style,* the *Associated Press Stylebook and Libel Manual,* and the *UPI Stylebook.* A magazine's editorial staff also uses a dictionary they have all agreed upon to consult for spelling and word use questions. *Merriam-Webster's Collegiate Dictionary* is a common choice.

had median annual salaries of $40,280 in 2002. Senior editors on large-circulation magazines earn much higher salaries.

Outlook

Magazine publishing is a dynamic industry. New magazines are launched almost every day of the year, and the majority of them fail. According to Magazine Publishers of America, 289 new magazines were introduced in 2002. A recent trend in magazine publishing is to focus on a special interest. There is increasing opportunity for employment at special-interest and trade magazines. Association magazines also offer promising employment opportunities.

Employment of editors is expected to increase about as fast as the average for all other occupations, especially at special-interest and professional association publications, but the field is very competitive.

FOR MORE INFO

For membership information, contact
American Society of Magazine Editors
810 Seventh Avenue, 24th Floor
New York, NY 10019
http://asme.magazine.org

For industry statistics, information on diversity, and to view a PowerPoint presentation entitled "Tips on Finding a Job in Magazines," visit the MPA website.
Magazine Publishers of America (MPA)
810 Seventh Avenue, 24th Floor
New York, NY 10019
Email: mpa@magazine.org
http://www.magazine.org

Newspaper Editors

What Newspaper Editors Do

Newspapers are an important means of communicating what happens in the world, from events in your own city or town to news from around the world. Your city's paper may cover different news items than a paper from another city and present stories from different points of view. *Newspaper editors* decide on the types of articles reporters will write. Because of the ever-changing nature of the news, newspaper editors work in a very hectic environment.

The newspaper staff might have many editors or just a few, depending on the size of the paper. The size of the paper often depends on the size of the city where the paper is published. The *editor in chief* or the *managing editor* directs the overall operation of the paper. He or she selects articles, assigns them to reporters and identifies their beats, meaning the special locations or subjects the reporters will cover.

Story editors, or *wire editors,* take news stories sent from large news agencies and choose which items to print in their own papers. Wire services provide smaller papers with stories from faraway places.

Franklin's Firsts

The first newspaper in the American colonies appeared in the early 18th century. It was Benjamin Franklin (1706–90) who, as editor and writer, made the *Pennsylvania Gazette* one of the most important in setting a high standard for other American journalists. Franklin also published the first magazine in the colonies, *The American Magazine,* in 1741.

A newspaper's own reporters turn in their stories to their *department editors*. These include business editors, sports editors, entertainment editors, fashion editors, and technology editors. Department editors are skilled writers as well as experts on their section's subject matter.

Department editors pass their approved articles on to the news editors, who arrange the articles and determine the layout of each page. They place the major news stories in the front of the paper with bigger headlines. Less important articles are placed farther from the front page. *News editors* give the articles to the copy desk, where copy editors check the text for completeness, spelling, grammar, and correct newspaper style. *Copy editors* often write the headlines, which are important for getting the reader's attention.

Production editors work closely with the people who place the advertisements to work out space for ads, news, features, and photographs.

Many newspapers have online versions that feature stories and information from the print edition, as well as original content. *Online editors* are responsible for the creation and organization of this online content.

Education and Training

Newspaper editors must know about many subjects and be able to express their ideas clearly. They must know about local, national, and international issues and be able to judge their importance and decide which stories to publish.

To prepare for a career as a newspaper editor, you should take high school courses in history, English, literature,

EXPLORING

- Keep a journal, focusing on writing about events during the day and describing them in detail. Try to rework your writing until it is as good as you can make it.
- Read all kinds of magazines and newspapers, including national newspapers.
- Work on a school newspaper or other publication.
- Ask your teacher to arrange an information interview with a newspaper editor.

Make It Simple

News writing should be correct, concise, and simple. One of the jobs of newspaper editors is to rewrite complex words, phrases, and sentences to make them short and to the point. For example, the phrases on the left could be changed to the ones on the right:

adverse weather conditions	bad weather
in the event of	if
take into custody	arrest
not yet known	unknown
assistance	help
not in favor of	opposes
finalize	end
take into consideration	consider
held a meeting	met
gave permission to	permitted

journalism, social science, computer science, and typing. You should attend college and take courses in the same subjects, as well as economics and political science. A bachelor's degree in journalism, English, communications, or one of the other liberal arts is required in this field, and a master's degree is usually helpful. When newspapers hire editors, they look closely at extracurricular activities, especially internships, school newspaper work, freelance writing and editing, and part-time newspaper work. Typing, computer skills, and knowledge of printing are helpful.

Earnings

Newspaper editors' salaries vary from small to large communities. Other factors affecting earnings include education, previous experience, job level, and the newspaper's circulation.

Large city dailies offer higher paying jobs, while outlying weekly papers pay less. According to the *Occupational Outlook Handbook,* salaries for all editors ranged from less than $24,010 to $76,620 or more in 2002. Newspaper editors earned median salaries of $46,410 in 2002. Senior editors at large newspapers earned higher salaries.

Outlook

Employment for newspaper editors should increase about as fast as the average over the next several years. However, because so many people are attracted to these jobs, competition will be stiff. It may be easier to find your first job with a small daily newspaper, although the pay will probably be lower.

FOR MORE INFO

To receive more information about a career as a newspaper editor, contact
American Society of Newspaper Editors
11690B Sunrise Valley Drive
Reston, VA 20191-1409
Tel: 703-453-1122
Email: asne@asne.org
http://www.asne.org

To read the Journalists Road to Success, *which presents an overview of careers and lists schools offering degrees in news-editorial, visit the DJNF website.*
Dow Jones Newspaper Fund (DJNF)
PO Box 300
Princeton, NJ 08543-0300
Email: newsfund@wsj.dowjones.com
http://djnewspaperfund.dowjones.com

For information on journalism careers, contact
Society of Professional Journalists
3909 North Meridian Street
Indianapolis, IN 46208
Tel: 317-927-8000
Email: questions@spj.org
http://www.spj.org

Visit the following website for comprehensive information on journalism careers, summer programs, and college journalism programs.
High School Journalism
http://www.highschooljournalism.org

Photographers

What Photographers Do

Photographers take pictures to record events, illustrate text, sell products, capture scenes, and for many other purposes. They are experts on cameras, lenses, filters, film, and lighting. To prepare to take pictures, photographers choose the right film for the lighting conditions. They choose lenses, such as a close-up lens or a wide-angle lens. They adjust all the settings on the camera, so that the right amount of light hits the film for the right amount of time when the shutter button is pressed. These decisions are technical and require some math ability, but they are also artistic decisions because small adjustments can give a great variety of special effects.

Photographers also know how to develop film and print pictures. They mix chemicals with precise measurements and soak the film in a series of mixtures for exact times. Once film is developed and dried, photographers place the film in enlargers that magnify the film. Lights in the enlarger shine through the film onto light-sensitive photographic paper. The paper is then soaked in a series of chemical baths, rinsed, and dried.

Profile: Ansel Adams (1902–84)

U.S. photographer Ansel Adams is known for his dramatic scenes of the American West and for his contributions to photographic technology. His zone system is a method of controlling film exposure and development to give a range of dark and light tones in black and white prints.

Adams was born in San Francisco. He studied music and photography and was a concert pianist until 1930. In 1932 he joined Edward Weston and other photographers in forming Group f/64, which helped establish photography as a fine art. Adams's photos were published in more than 35 books and portfolios. He also wrote many books on photographic techniques, including *The Negative* and *The Print*.

Photographers often specialize in one kind of photography. For example, *photojournalists* take pictures of events, people, places, or things for newspapers, Internet sites, and magazines. (See the sidebar "What Photojournalists Do" for more information.) *Portrait photographers* take pictures of people in their own studios, or at schools, homes, weddings, and parties. *Commercial photographers* take pictures of products, fashions, food, or machinery. *Aerial photographers* take pictures from airplanes for newspapers, businesses, research companies, or the military. *Scientific photographers* take pictures for scientific magazines and books. *Fine art photographers* take pictures for artistic expression. They might shoot images that are beautiful, thought provoking, or even disturbing to convey ideas and feelings.

Digital photography is a relatively new development. With this new technology, film is replaced by microchips that record pictures in digital format. Pictures can then be downloaded onto a computer's hard drive. Photographers use special software to manipulate the images on screen. Digital photography is used primarily for electronic publishing and advertising.

EXPLORING

- Experiment with different cameras, films, digital photography, and subject matter. Take photos of friends and family, school events, current events in your town, objects, landscapes, animals, or buildings.
- Join school camera clubs, or work on your yearbook or newspaper staff.
- Enter contests sponsored by magazines or community groups.
- Explore your local library or bookstore and the Internet. Look for information on how to compose photos, arrange lighting, determine camera settings, and choose film for various effects.

Education and Training

Classes in photography, chemistry, and art will help prepare you for this career. If you are interested in digital photography, study computers and learn how to use programs that manipulate photos.

You do not have to earn a college degree to become a photographer, but many colleges offer a bachelor's degree in photography. A college program will teach you advanced techniques and help you build a portfolio of your work.

Earnings

Salaried photographers earned salaries that ranged from less than $14,640 to $49,920 or more in 2002, according to the *Occupational Outlook Handbook*. Photographers employed by book, newspaper, and directory publishers earned median salaries of $35,630 in 2002.

Many photographers are self-employed freelancers. They often earn more than those on salary, but their

Photographers often work outdoors in a wide variety of weather conditions. (Photodisc)

What Photojournalists Do

Photojournalists shoot photographs that capture news events. Their job is to tell a story with pictures. They may cover a war in Central America, the Olympics, a national election, or a small town Fourth of July parade. In addition to shooting pictures, they also write captions or other supporting text. Photojournalists may also develop and print photographs or edit film. More and more photojournalists are using digital photography, particularly for foreign assignments, since the electronic images can be sent instantly by computer modem or other forms of electronic transmission.

Photojournalists are employed by newspapers, magazines, and other print publications. They may also work for online publications. Many work as freelancers who research their own stories, document them, and sell them to various print media.

earnings can go up and down depending on how much work is available.

Outlook

Employment of photographers will increase about as fast as the average over the next several years. As more newspapers and magazines turn to electronic publishing, more photographers will be needed to provide digital images. Outside the publishing industry, portrait photographers should enjoy strong employment prospects due to population increases.

FOR MORE INFO

For information on careers in photography and education, contact
American Society of Media Photographers
150 North Second Street
Philadelphia, PA 19106
Tel: 215-451-2769
http://www.asmp.org

For information on careers in photojournalism, contact
National Press Photographers Association
3200 Croasdaile Drive, Suite 306
Durham, NC 27705
Tel: 919-383-7246
Email: info@nppa.org
http://www.nppa.org

For information on training and their monthly magazine, contact
Professional Photographers of America
229 Peachtree Street, NE, Suite 2200
Atlanta, GA 30303
Tel: 800-786-6277
http://www.ppa.com

For information on student membership, contact
Student Photographic Society
229 Peachtree Street, NE, Suite 2200
Atlanta, GA 30303
Tel: 800-339-5451, ext. 237
Email: info@studentphoto.com
http://www.studentphoto.com

Prepress Workers

What Prepress Workers Do

Prepress workers arrange and prepare the text and pictures that eventually become newspapers, magazines, books, and other printed materials. They work in commercial printing, business printing, newspaper printing, and printing trade service firms.

A variety of prepress careers are available. Some are skilled crafts that take years to master, but most prepress work now is computer-based and requires a high degree of computer literacy.

Compositors and *typesetters* set and arrange type for printing, either by hand or electronically (such as phototypesetting). *Paste-up workers* position illustrations and lay out columns of type.

Once the final version of a page has been assembled, a photographic negative of the page is made. Film negatives are most commonly produced directly from the computer. If they are not, or if camera-ready art is involved, a *camera operator* photographs the material and develops a negative.

The *film stripper* makes any last-minute changes and assembles the different pieces of film into position. The *platemaker*, often called a *lithographer*, then makes the printing plate from the film negative. The plate is what goes into the printing press.

Manual prepress work is being phased out by *desktop publishing specialists*, who typeset, lay out, and

To Be a Successful Prepress Worker, You Should . . .

○ have strong communication skills
○ be attentive to detail
○ have the ability to perform well in a high-pressure, deadline-driven environment
○ possess good manual dexterity, eyesight, and overall visual perception
○ have artistic skill

EXPLORING

○ Obtain a summer job or internship doing basic word processing or desktop publishing tasks.
○ Volunteer to do desktop publishing or design work for your school newspaper or yearbook.
○ Ask your teacher or guidance counselor to arrange a tour of a printing plant.

design text and graphics on a personal computer. In this process, all the elements on screen appear exactly as they will in the printed piece. (See the chapter on desktop publishing specialists for more information.) Camera-ready photos and art are scanned by the *scanner operator*, who converts them into electronic images that can be added to a file.

Electronic files are reviewed by *pre-flight technicians* to ensure that all the elements are properly formatted and set up.

Education and Training

Educational requirements for prepress workers vary by duty, but most prepress jobs require at least a high school diploma. Recommended high school courses include English, computer science, mathematics, photography, chemistry, physics, drawing, and art.

The more traditional jobs, such as camera operator, film stripper, lithographic artist, and platemaker, require longer, more specialized preparation. This might involve an apprenticeship or an associate's degree. But these jobs now are on the decline, as they are being replaced by computerized processes.

Postsecondary education is strongly encouraged for most prepress positions and is a requirement for some jobs, such as managerial positions. Graphic arts programs are offered by community and junior colleges as well as four-year colleges and universities. Postsecondary programs in printing technology are also available.

Any programs or courses that give you exposure to the printing field will be an asset. Courses in printing are often available at vocational-technical institutes and through printing trade associations.

Earnings

Pay rates vary for prepress workers, depending on their level of experience and responsibility, type of company, where they live, and whether or not they are union members. Salaries for prepress workers ranged from less than $18,050 to $50,660 or more annually in 2002, according to the U.S. Department of Labor. The median salary for prepress workers was $31,150 in 2002.

Outlook

Overall employment in the prepress portion of the printing industry is expected to decline over the next decade. While it is anticipated that the demand for printed materials will increase, the demand for prepress work will not, mainly because of new innovations.

Almost all prepress operations are computerized, and many of the traditional jobs that involved highly skilled handwork—film strippers, paste-up workers, and platemakers—are being

---

Did You Know?

- Printing is the third largest manufacturing industry in the United States.
- Approximately 56,000 prepress workers are employed in the United States.
- Illinois, Wisconsin, Minnesota, Maryland, and Kansas employ the highest number of prepress workers.

Sources: Graphic Arts Information Network, U.S. Department of Labor

phased out. The computer-oriented aspects of prepress work have replaced most of these tasks. Employment growth for desktop publishing specialists, however, is expected to be faster than the average. Specialized computer skills will increasingly be needed to handle direct-to-plate and other new prepress technologies.

FOR MORE INFO

For information on education and training programs available through local union schools, contact
Graphic Communications International Union
1900 L Street, NW
Washington, DC 20036
Tel: 202-462-1400
http://www.gciu.org

For information on the career of prepress worker, visit the GAIN website.
(GAIN) Graphic Arts Information Network
http://www.gain.net/PIA_GATF/learning_center/prepress.html

For comprehensive educational and career information about the graphic communications industry, visit
Graphic Comm Central
http://teched.vt.edu/gcc

Printing Press Workers

What Printing Press Workers Do

Today's printing presses are much faster than they used to be, and most are controlled by computers. Some presses can print nearly 150,000 newspapers an hour. Running these fast, modern presses is the job of *printing press operators* and their assistants.

These workers set up, operate, clean, and maintain presses. The web press is the most common press used for printing newspapers, magazines, and books. With a web press, the ink is on a revolving cylinder that prints onto a continuous sheet of paper (the web) coming off a giant roll. The other type of press is a sheet-fed press, which prints on single sheets of paper rather than on a continuous roll.

Press operators first prepare the press. They inspect and oil the moving parts and clean and adjust the ink rollers and ink fountains. When they receive the printing plates from the prepress area, they mount them into place on the printing surface or cylinder. They mix and match the ink, fill the ink fountains, and adjust the ink flow and dampening systems. They also load the paper, adjust the press to the paper size, feed the paper through the cylinders and, on a web press, adjust the tension controls. When this is done, a proof sheet is run off for the customer's review.

> **Median Hourly Wages for Printing Press Workers by Industry, 2002**
>
> ○ Newspapers, periodicals, book, and directory publishers: $16.09
> ○ Commercial printing: $15.02
> ○ Converted paper products: $14.95
> ○ Plastic products: $13.21
> ○ Business support services: $10.60
>
> Source: U.S. Department of Labor

A printing press operator checks a page for quality during the printing process. (R. R. Donnelley & Sons)

When the proof has been approved and final adjustments have been made, the press run begins. During the run, press operators constantly check the quality of the printed sheets and make any necessary adjustments. They make sure the print is clear and properly positioned and that ink is not blotting onto other sheets. If the job involves color, they make sure that the colors line up properly. Operators also monitor the chemical properties of the ink and correct temperatures in the drying chamber, if the press has one. On a web press, the feeding and tension mechanisms must be continually monitored. If the paper tears or jams, it must be rethreaded. As a roll of paper runs out, a new one must be spliced onto the old one.

When the press run is finished, the press operators clean and check the press so that it is ready for another printing job.

EXPLORING

- Take print shop classes, which provide the most direct exposure to this work.
- Work on your school newspaper or yearbook to learn more about the printing process.
- Visit a local printing plant to see presses in action and get a feel for the environment in which press operators work.
- Try to get a part-time, temporary, or summer job as a cleanup worker or press feeder in a printing plant.

Strong communication skills, both verbal and written, are a must for press operators and assistants. They also must be able to work well as a team, both with each other and with others in the printing company. Any miscommunication during the printing process can be costly if it means rerunning a job or any part of it. Working well under pressure is another requirement because most print jobs run on tight deadlines.

Education and Training

A high school diploma is the minimum education required for a position as a printing press operator. Classes in art, print shop, mathematics, chemistry, physics, and computer science

---

A Brief History of Printing

A.D. 105	Paper was invented in China by Ts'ai Lun.
868	The first known book was printed in China using wood blocks and ink.
1045	The earliest known movable type (made of clay) was developed by Pi Sheng in China.
1440s	Johannes Gutenberg invented movable type in metal in conjunction with a wooden printing press. This revolutionized the printing process.
Late 1700s	Lithography is invented by a German named Aloys Senefelder. Lithography is a printing process by which the plate, or image-carrier, is chemically treated so that the areas to be printed hold ink and the non-image areas repel ink.
1800s	The rotary press, which used revolving cylinders to make an inked impression on paper; the Linotype and the Monotype machines, which automated the process of setting type, were invented.
1905	American Ira Rubel discovered offset printing—the predominant method of printing today.
1930s	Four-color printing becomes commonplace.
1960s	Electronic typesetting introduced.
1980s	Personal computers and desktop publishing become popular and allow users to typeset and design entire pages on their computer screens.
1990s	Computer-to-plate printing is developed.

are helpful. Computer training is essential for anyone entering the field. An apprenticeship or postsecondary training in a vocational-technical or graphic arts program is strongly recommended.

Earnings

Pay rates vary for printing press workers, depending on their level of experience and responsibility, type of company, where they live, and whether or not they are union members. Median hourly earnings for printing press operators were $13.95 (or $29,016 annually) in 2002, according to the U.S. Department of Labor. Salaries ranged from less than $8.32 an hour ($17,306 annually) to $22.46 ($46,717 annually) or more an hour.

Outlook

Employment growth for press operators is expected to be slower than the average in the next decade. Today's larger more efficient machines require fewer workers to handle the increased demand for printed materials, such as advertising, direct mail pieces, computer software packaging, books, and magazines.

Newcomers to the field are likely to encounter stiff competition from experienced workers or workers who have completed retraining programs to update their skills. Opportunities are expected to be greatest for people who have completed formal apprenticeships or postsecondary training programs.

FOR MORE INFO

For information on education and training programs available through local union schools, contact

Graphic Communications International Union
1900 L Street, NW
Washington, DC 20036
Tel: 202-462-1400
http://www.gciu.org

For information and skills standards and certification for printing press workers, contact

National Council for Skill Standards in Graphic Communications
Harry V. Quadracci Printing & Graphic Center
800 Main Street
Pewaukee, WI 53072
Tel: 262-695-3470
http://www.ncssgc.org

For comprehensive educational and career information about the graphic communications industry, visit

Graphic Comm Central
http://teched.vt.edu/gcc

Reporters

What Reporters Do

Reporters gather information and report the news for magazines and newspapers. (They also work for radio and television stations, but this article focuses on reporters who work in print journalism.) Reports cover stories on local, national, or international events. *Correspondents* cover stories from a specific city or country.

Reporters and correspondents gather all the information they need to write clear and accurate news stories. They interview people, research the facts and history behind a story, observe important events, and then write the story. News stories may be a one-day item, or they become a series that follows an event over several days or weeks.

Many newspaper, wire service, and magazine reporters specialize in one type of story. *Topical reporters* cover stories for a specific department, such as medicine, politics, or sports. *Feature writers* generally write longer stories than news reporters, usually

The All-Important Interview

Good reporters are usually good interviewers. They interview experts to get the details of a story. For example, they might talk to an oncologist about a new cancer treatment. Reporters interview eyewitnesses, such as customers who saw a bank robber, or people who lived through a hurricane. They interview people to get their opinions on news events, such as citizens who might be affected by the construction of a highway through their neighborhood. Interviews are important for getting the facts, supporting the facts, and getting various sides of the story. Take a look at your local newspaper or a national news magazine. How many stories use interviews? What questions did the reporters ask? Did the interviews supply important information? Would the story have been as good without the interviews?

on upbeat subjects such as fashion, art, or social events. *Editorial writers* and *syndicated news columnists* present viewpoints that, although based on a thorough knowledge, are opinions on topics of popular interest. *Columnists* write under a byline and usually specialize in a particular subject, such as politics or government activities. They often give their personal opinions about an issue.

To gather information, all reporters take notes and record or videotape interviews with news sources. Reporters may also examine documents related to the story. Before reporters start putting together their stories, they discuss the importance of the subject matter with a *newspaper editor*. Editors decide what news will be covered each day. They determine how long a story should be and how much importance to give it. Sometimes they decide to hold the story for a while or not to run it at all.

Reporters then organize the information and write a concise, informative story. Reporters and correspondents who are too far from their editorial office to return to file their reports may phone, email, or fax it in.

Because of continual deadline pressure, a reporter's life is hectic. Newspaper articles must be filed long before the first edition is printed, which is usually in the very early hours of the morning. If a major news story takes place, reporters may have to work 18 or 20 hours without a break.

Some correspondents are assigned to cover dangerous areas. War stories are frequently filed from the country where the war is taking place. Reporters who cover riots, floods, major disasters, and other stories must be able to work in difficult, dangerous, and upsetting situations.

EXPLORING

○ Work on your school newspaper or on a church, synagogue, or mosque newsletter. You can offer to be a reporter or writer, or you can help with word processing and printing.
○ Read your local newspaper regularly. Follow the work of one or two reporters who cover a topic that interests you.
○ Ask your teacher to set up an information interview with a newspaper or magazine reporter.

Education and Training

You can begin to prepare for a career as a reporter in high school. Take courses in English, writing, history, typing, and computer science. After high school, you should go to college and earn a bachelor's degree. Your degree can be in journalism or liberal arts. Master's degrees are becoming more important for journalists, particularly for teachers and specialists.

If you plan to specialize in a particular subject, such as science writing, it is important to take several courses in that subject.

Earnings

Salaries for entry-level reporters at newspapers range from $10,000 to $25,000 a year, depending on the size of the publication and its location. Newspaper reporters earned mean annual salaries of $35,740 in 2002, according to the U.S. Department of Labor. Experienced newspaper reporters can earn between $18,000 and $70,000 a year.

Profile: Nellie Bly

Nellie Bly (1865–1922) was the first woman to become famous as a reporter. She was one of the most adventurous journalists of the 19th century. She became world-renowned because of a 72-day trip around the world she took to beat the fictional record set by Phineas Fogg in Jules Verne's *Around the World in 80 Days*.

Bly was born Elizabeth Cochran in Cochran Mills, Pennsylvania. She received most of her education at home, spending only one year in school. In 1885, she began her career in journalism as a reporter for the *Pittsburgh Dispatch,* where she began to use the pseudonym Nellie Bly. In 1887, she joined Joseph Pulitzer's *New York World*. She wrote about social issues, and many of her articles were the result of undercover investigations she conducted. In 1895, Bly married Robert L. Seaman and retired to private life. In 1919, she returned to reporting with the *New York Journal,* and she remained there until her death.

Outlook

Employment for reporters and correspondents is expected to grow more slowly than the average over the next decade. Mergers, consolidations, closures, and decreasing circulation have reduced the number of opportunities available in the newspaper industry. Online newspapers and magazines may offer better opportunities for reporters. Opportunities will be slightly better at magazines, but these positions are highly sought after, so competition is stiff. Beginning journalists will find more jobs in small towns or at smaller publications. Some major daily newspapers offer a limited number of one-year, full-time internships for aspiring new reporters, with no guarantee that they will be kept on afterward.

FOR MORE INFO

For information on careers in nonfiction writing, contact
American Society of Journalists and Authors
1501 Broadway, Suite 302
New York, NY 10036
Tel: 212-997-0947
http://www.asja.org

For general educational information on all areas of journalism (newspapers, magazines, television, radio, and the Internet), contact
Association for Education in Journalism and Mass Communication
234 Outlet Pointe Boulevard
Columbia, SC 29210-5667
Tel: 803-798-0271
http://www.aejmc.org

For information on careers in the newspaper industry, contact
Dow Jones Newspaper Fund
PO Box 300
Princeton, NJ 08543-0300
Email: newsfund@wsj.dowjones.com
http://djnewspaperfund.dowjones.com

For information on journalism careers, contact
Society of Professional Journalists
3909 North Meridian Street
Indianapolis, IN 46208
Tel: 317-927-8000
Email: questions@spj.org
http://www.spj.org

Visit the following website for comprehensive information on journalism careers, summer programs, and college journalism programs.
High School Journalism
http://www.highschooljournalism.org

Science and Medical Writers

What Science and Medical Writers Do

Science and medical writers research, interpret, write, and edit scientific and medical information. They translate complex information into terms that the general public and professionals in the field easily understand. Their work appears in books, technical studies and reports, on websites, in newspapers and magazines, and may be used for radio and television broadcasts.

A science or medical writer may write about a new drug made by a pharmaceutical company. Research facilities employ these writers to edit reports or write about their scientific or medical studies. Science and medical writers may work as *public information officers* writing press releases that inform the

Science and Medical Writers by a Different Name

Medical and science writers can have many different job titles, such as the following:

- health writer
- science writer
- health specialist
- technical writer
- clinical research specialist
- medical information specialist
- communications specialist
- drug information specialist
- pharmaceutical information officer
- health or science editor
- biomedical writer
- online medical writer

> ## EXPLORING
>
> ○ You are a medical writer and you write an article about a health problem or safety situation that might affect children. Think of all the people who might be interested in your article. Who might benefit from the information in your article? These are just a few: nurses and doctors, school administrators, hospital workers, insurance agents, school bus drivers, lawyers, teachers.
>
> ○ Read about developments in research for a cure to a disease or a new drug. Read about the same topic in a general news magazine and in a scientific journal. How do the writers make the information easier for the general public to understand?

public about the latest scientific or medical research findings. Educational publishers hire science and medical writers to write or edit educational materials for the medical profession. Or that same publisher may hire writers to write online articles or interactive courses that are distributed over the Internet.

Science and medical writers must ask a lot of questions and enjoy hunting for information that might add to the article. They do hours of research on the Internet or in libraries. Sometimes writers interview professionals such as doctors, pharmacists, scientists, engineers, managers, and others professionals.

Some medical and science writers specialize in their subject matter. For instance, a medical writer may write only about heart disease. Science writers may limit their writing or focus on only one subject such as air-pollution issues.

Education and Training

If you are considering a career as a writer, you should take many English and writing classes. Computer classes will also be helpful. If you know in high school that you want to do scientific or medical writing, you should take biology, physiology, chemistry, physics, math, health, and other science courses.

Not all writers are college educated, but employers almost always require applicants to have a bachelor's degree. Many writers earn an undergraduate degree in English, journalism, or liberal arts and then obtain a master's degree in a communications field such as medical or science writing.

If you are considering a career as a medical or science writer, you should enjoy writing, be able to write well, and be able to express your ideas and those of others clearly. You should learn all about the English language and work hard on your grammar and spelling skills. You should be a curious person, enjoy learning about new things, and have an interest in science or medicine.

Earnings

There are no specific salary studies for science and medical writers. The U.S. Department of Labor reports that all writers earned salaries that ranged from less than $21,320 to more

Questions and More Questions

As a science or medical writer, you might be asked to report on a new heart surgery procedure that will soon be available to the public. You will need to find answers to questions like these:

- How is the surgery performed?
- What areas of the heart are affected?
- How does a healthy heart work and how does a diseased heart work in comparison?
- How will this surgery help the patient?
- How many people are affected by this disease?
- What are the symptoms?
- How many procedures have been done successfully?
- Where were the procedures performed?
- What is the recovery time?
- Are there are any complications?

In addition, interviews with doctors and patients will add a personal touch to your story.

FOR MORE INFO

For information on a career as a medical writer, contact

American Medical Writers Association
40 West Gude Drive, Suite 101
Rockville, MD 20850-1192
Tel: 301-294-5303
Email: amwa@amwa.org
http://www.amwa.org

To read advice for beginning science writers, visit the NASW website.

National Association of Science Writers (NASW)
PO Box 890
Hedgesville, WV 25427
Tel: 304-754-5077
http://www.nasw.org

For information on careers in technical communication and a database of academic programs, visit the STC website.

Society for Technical Communication (STC)
901 North Stuart Street, Suite 904
Arlington, VA 22203
Tel: 703-522-4114
Email: stc@stc.org
http://www.stc.org

than $85,150 in 2002. Writers who are employed by the publishing industry earned average salaries of $33,550 in 2002.

Outlook

There is a lot of competition for writing jobs and employment for all writers is expected to grow at an average rate over the next decade. The Society for Technical Communication says there is a growing demand for technical communicators. They report that it is one of the fastest growing professions and that this growth has created a variety of career options. As there are more advances in medicine and science, there will continue to be a need for skilled writers to provide that information to the public and other professionals.

Technical Writers and Editors

What Technical Writers and Editors Do

Technical writers put scientific and technical information into understandable language. They write manuals, technical reports, sales proposals, and scripts for audiovisual and video programs. The manuals that they prepare give instructions on how to install, assemble, use, or repair products or equipment. These manuals can be as simple as instructions on how to assemble a bicycle or as complex as instructions on how to operate a nuclear generator. Computer manuals are the most common types of manuals prepared by technical writers.

Technical editors work with writers to correct any errors in written material and to make text flow more clearly. They also may coordinate writing projects and arrange for graphic designers and technical illustrators to produce artwork.

Before technical writers begin writing, they gather as much information as possible about the subject. They read and review all available materials, including engineering drawings, reports, and journal articles. Technical writers interview people familiar with the topic, such as engineers, scientists, and computer

---

Did You Know?

○ Approximately 44,780 technical writers are employed in the United States.
○ Washington, Massachusetts, and Colorado employ the highest number of technical writers.
○ More than one-third of all writers and editors are self-employed.

Source: U.S. Department of Labor

programmers. Once they have gathered the necessary information, they write a first draft.

The writer gives copies of the rough draft to the technical editor and engineers to review. The technical editor corrects any errors in spelling, punctuation, and grammar and checks that all parts of the document are clear and understandable. The writer revises the rough draft based on comments from the engineers and the editor. The technical editor again checks the final copy to make sure that all pictures are properly placed, that captions match the correct pictures, and that there are no other errors.

In addition to traditional books and paper documents, technical writers and editors prepare materials for CD-ROMs, multimedia programs, and the Web.

Education and Training

If you are interested in becoming a technical writer or editor, you should understand complex scientific ideas and be able to explain them to others. In high school, take as many English and science classes as you can. Business, journalism, math, and computer classes will also be helpful.

You will need to earn a bachelor's degree to get a job in this field. Many technical writers earn degrees in engineering or science and take technical writing classes. Technical editors may earn degrees in English or journalism. Many technical writers and editors earn advanced degrees, such as master's degrees. Writers and editors need to pursue learning throughout their careers to find out about new technologies, such as desktop publishing or creating multimedia programs.

Many technical writers start their careers as scientists, engineers, or technicians and move into writing after a few years. Technical editors may start out as editorial assistants or proofreaders and advance to an editorial position once they have more experience.

Earnings

Median annual earnings for salaried technical writers employed by the newspaper, book, and directory publishing industries were $42,950 in 2002, according to the U.S. Department of Labor. Salaries for all technical writers ranged from less than $30,270 to more than $80,900. Editors employed by the publishing industry earned average annual salaries of $46,410 in 2002. Salaries for all editors ranged from less than $24,010 to $76,620 or more annually.

Outlook

The writing and editing field is generally very competitive. Each year, there are more people trying to enter this field than there are

EXPLORING

- Work on a literary magazine, student newspaper, or yearbook.
- Learn a new computer program or language by using a computer manual. How informative or easy to follow are the author's instructions?
- Read all sorts of books, magazines, and newspapers. This will expose you to both good and bad writing styles and techniques and help you to identify why one approach works better than another.

Read All about it

Alred, Gerald J., Charles T. Brusaw, and Walter E. Oliu. *The Technical Writer's Companion.* 3rd ed. Boston, Mass.: Bedford/St. Martin's, 2002.

Blake, Gary, and Robert W. Bly. *The Elements of Technical Writing.* Upper Saddle River, N.J.: Pearson Higher Education, 2000.

Gould, Jay Reid, Wayne A. Losano, Blythe Camenson, and Jim Cochran. *Opportunities in Technical Writing Careers.* New York: McGraw-Hill/Contemporary Books, 2000.

Young, Matt. *Technical Writer's Handbook: Writing with Style and Clarity.* Sausalito, Calif.: University Science Books, 2002.

FOR MORE INFO

For information on science writing, contact
National Association of Science Writers
PO Box 890
Hedgesville, WV 25427
Tel: 304-754-5077
http://www.nasw.org

For information on careers in technical communication, contact
Society for Technical Communication
901 North Stuart Street, Suite 904
Arlington, VA 22203
Tel: 703-522-4114
Email: stc@stc.org
http://www.stc.org

available openings. The field of technical writing and editing, though, offers more opportunities than other areas of writing and editing, such as book publishing or journalism. Employment opportunities for technical writers and editors are expected to grow faster than the average over the next decade. Demand is growing for technical writers who can produce well-written computer manuals. The need for technical writers in the pharmaceutical industry is also growing. Rapid growth in the technology and electronics industries and the Internet will create a continuing demand for people to write users' guides, instruction manuals, and training materials.

Webmasters

What Webmasters Do

Webmasters create and manage websites for large corporations (such as publishing companies), small businesses, nonprofit organizations, government agencies, schools, and other groups.

Some webmasters develop the content for the pages they manage. They may write the text or receive it from other writers and editors. Webmasters insert codes into the text in HyperText Markup Language (HTML). HTML code tells the computer how to arrange and format the text. Webmasters also select images and scan them into the document. Images are also coded with HTML so that they appear in the desired size and position.

Many websites contain information that changes regularly. An organization may make changes once a month. A newspaper may post updates several times in one day. Webmasters maintain and update websites, inserting current data.

Websites usually have links to other pages or other websites. Webmasters check the links and make sure visitors to the site can connect easily to the information they need.

Webmasters also keep track of activity to the site. They note how often people visit their site. They answer questions and comments from visitors, usually by email. Some webmasters are in charge of processing customer orders for products or services.

Web Growth in Number of Sites

Year	Sites
1998	2,636,000
1999	4,662,000
2002	9,040,000

Source: Online Computer Library Center

EXPLORING

○ Spend time surfing the Web. Look at a variety of websites to see how they look and operate.
○ Design a Web page. Many Internet providers offer their users the option of designing and maintaining a personal Web page for a very low fee. A personal page can contain virtually anything that you want to include—snapshots of friends, audio files of favorite music, or links to other favorite sites.
○ Ask your teacher to set up an information interview with a webmaster.

Education and Training

If you are interested in becoming a webmaster, take as many computer science classes as you can in high school. Mathematics classes will also be helpful. Finally, take English and writing classes, since writing skills are important in this career.

Many webmasters have bachelor's degrees in liberal arts, engineering, or computer science. Others have two-year degrees from a technical or vocational school.

Most people who enter this field have a background in computer technology. When considering candidates for the position of webmaster, employers usually look for at least two years of experience with various Web technologies, including knowl-

Spinning the Web

The Internet developed from ARPANET, an experimental computer network established in the 1960s by the U.S. Department of Defense. By the late 1980s, the Internet was being used by many government and educational institutions. In the early 1990s public use of the Internet increased dramatically, spurred by the development of the Web.

The Web had its beginnings in 1991, when hypertext code was developed. In 1993, the first Web browser, Mosaic, became available, developed by programmers at the University of Illinois. Businesses quickly realized the commercial potential of the Web and soon developed their own Web sites. By early 1998, the number of websites on the Internet had grown to 2,636,000. According to the Online Computer Library Center, the Web contained 9,040,000 unique sites in 2002.

> ## Words to Learn
>
> **browser** a program designed to read and display HTML-encoded documents and to use the transmission protocols used by the World Wide Web; the top-two browsers are Microsoft Internet Explorer and Netscape Navigator
>
> **homepage** a Web page that introduces the site and guides the user to other pages at the site
>
> **HTML (HyperText Markup Language)** a code that helps control the way information on a Web page is transferred and presented and the way that hypertext links appear on the page
>
> **search engine** a specialized website containing computer-maintained lists of other web sites; lists are usually organized by subject, name, content, and other categories; users request searches by typing in keywords, or topical words and phrases, and the search engine displays a list of links to related websites
>
> **Web page** an Internet document; it is typically a hypertext document, meaning that it provides links to related Web pages, either on the same website or on another website
>
> **website** an Internet resource that contains one or more Web pages

edge of HTML, JavaScript, and SQL. It is quite common for someone to move into the position of webmaster from another computer-related job in the same organization.

Earnings

According to Salary.com, the average salary for webmasters in 2004 was $61,797. Salaries ranged from $52,016 to $74,348. Many webmasters, however, move into their positions from another position within their company or perform webmaster duties in addition to other duties. These employees tend to receive lower salaries.

FOR MORE INFO

For information on schools that offer webmaster training, webmaster specialties, and a certification program, contact

International Webmasters Association
119 East Union Street, Suite F
Pasadena, CA 91103
Tel: 626-449-3709
http://www.iwanet.org

For career, education, and certification information, contact

World Organization of Webmasters
9580 Oak Avenue Parkway, Suite 7-177
Folsom, CA 95630
Tel: 916-608-1597
Email: info@joinwow.org
http://www.joinwow.org

According to the National Association of Colleges and Employers, the average starting salary for graduates with a bachelor's degree in computer science was $47,109 in 2003; in computer programming, $45,346; and in information sciences and systems, $38,282.

Outlook

According to the U.S. Department of Labor, the field of computer and data processing services is projected to be one of the fastest growing industries for the next decade. As a result, the employment rate of webmasters and other computer specialists is expected to grow much faster than the average rate for all occupations through 2012. The World Organization of Webmasters predicts that the growth of e-commerce and the emergence of new Web authoring tools will create demand for webmasters.

Writers

What Writers Do

Writers express their ideas in words for books, magazines, newspapers, advertisements, radio, television, and the Internet. Writers' jobs are a combination of creativity and hard work.

Writers usually specialize in a particular type of writing. For example, *newswriters* prepare stories for newspapers, radio, and TV. *Columnists* specialize in writing about matters from their personal viewpoints. *Critics* review and comment upon the work of other authors, musicians, artists, and performers.

Technical writers express technical and scientific ideas in easy-to-understand language. In addition to all of these types of writers, there are also creative writers, including *novelists, biographers, poets, essayists, comedy writers,* and *short story writers.*

Creative writers usually do not work on assignment, but choose their own topics and styles. Creative writers are somewhat different in this regard from journalists, copywriters, and

Where Do Writers Work?

According to the *Occupational Outlook Handbook,* more than 50 percent of salaried writers work for newspaper, magazine, book, and directory publishers; television and radio stations; software publishers; film studios; sound recording companies; and Internet companies. Writers are also employed by advertising agencies, companies that design computer systems, public relations firms, government agencies, and professional, business, labor, and political organizations.

others who are normally assigned topics by editors or publishers.

Many writers work outside the realm of publishing. Those who prepare scripts for motion pictures or television are called *screenwriters* or *scriptwriters*. *Playwrights* do similar writing but for theater. Those who write copy for advertisements are called *copywriters*.

Good writers gather as much information as possible about a subject and then carefully check the accuracy of their sources. This can involve extensive library research, interviews, and long hours of observation and personal experience. Writers keep notes from which they prepare an outline or summary. They write a first draft and then rewrite sections of the material, always searching for the best way to express an idea or opinion. A manuscript is reviewed, corrected, and revised many times before a final copy is ready.

Education and Training

In high school, take courses in English, literature, foreign languages, history, general science, social studies, computer science, and typing.

A college education is usually necessary if you want to become a writer. You should also know how to use a computer for word processing and be able to handle the pressure of deadlines. Some employers prefer to hire people who have a commu-

EXPLORING

- Read all kinds of writing—fiction, nonfiction, poetry, essays. Read books, newspapers, and magazines.
- Work as a reporter or writer on your school newspaper, yearbook, or literary magazine.
- Write every day. Keep a separate notebook just for journal writing. Here are some tips:
  - Set aside the same time every day to write in your journal. Try not to skip days.
  - Do not make writing a chore. Enjoy it! Think of it as having a conversation with yourself or an imaginary listener.
  - Remember that journal writing must not be perfect. Try not to worry about grammar, punctuation, and spelling. The important thing is to express yourself freely. Your journal is private and you do not need to show it to anyone else.

nications or journalism degree. Others require majors in English, literature, history, philosophy, or one of the social sciences. Technical writers should have a background in engineering, business, computers, or one of the sciences.

Many novelists, poets, playwrights, and short story writers learn their skills on their own. A few become successful without a college education, but most have attended at least some college-level courses. Classes and writing groups can be found almost anywhere, from community colleges to park districts to the Web.

A writer works on a manuscript in his home office. (Photodisc)

Earnings

Salaries for writers ranged from less than $21,320 to more than $85,140 in 2002, according to the U.S. Department of Labor. The median annual salary for writers employed by the newspaper, book, and directory publishing industries was $40,910

What Should I Write About?

You sit down to write and just cannot get started. If you have run out of ideas, try these exercises:

- Pretend you are a lion in a zoo watching people watching you. Describe what you see. What are you thinking?
- You have just landed on an unknown planet. What do you see?
- Find an interesting newspaper or magazine article. Describe what the article is about. Do you agree or disagree with the author? Why? How would you write the article differently?
- You are walking down the street and see a yellowed piece of paper with some strange writing on it. What happens next?

in 2002. Best-selling authors may make well over $200,000 per year, but they are few in number.

It is difficult to earn a living as a creative writer. Only a few become well-known enough to support themselves with their writing alone. Many creative writers work at other jobs and pursue creative writing on a part-time basis. Some authors get grants to allow them to do their writing. Others win prizes and awards.

Outlook

Employment opportunities in writing are expected to be good over the next decade. Jobs should be available at newspapers, magazines, book publishers, advertising agencies, businesses, and nonprofit organizations. Opportunities are expected to be especially good for technical writers. However, competition for jobs is very intense.

The job market for creative writers is difficult to predict. Their success depends on the amount and type of work they create and their ability to sell that work.

FOR MORE INFO

Information on writing and editing careers in the field of communications is available from

National Association of Science Writers
PO Box 890
Hedgesville, WV 25427
Tel: 304-754-5077
http://www.nasw.org

For information about working as a writer and union membership, contact

National Writers Union
113 University Place, 6th Floor
New York, NY 10003
Tel: 212-254-0279
Email: nwu@nwu.org
http://www.nwu.org

This organization offers student memberships for those interested in opinion writing.

National Conference of Editorial Writers
3899 North Front Street
Harrisburg, PA 17110
Tel: 717-703-3015
Email: ncew@pa-news.org
http://www.ncew.org

For information on careers in technical communication, contact

Society for Technical Communication
901 North Stuart Street, Suite 904
Arlington, VA 22203
Tel: 703-522-4114
Email: stc@stc.org
http://www.stc.org

Glossary

accredited   approved as meeting established standards for providing good training and education; this approval is usually given to a school or a program in a school by an independent organization of professionals

apprentice   person who is learning a trade by working under the supervision of a skilled worker; apprentices often receive classroom instruction in addition to their supervised practical experience

associate's degree   academic rank or title granted by a community or junior college or similar institution to graduates of a two-year program of education beyond high school

bachelor's degree   academic rank or title given to a person who has completed a four-year program of study at a college or university; also called an undergraduate degree or baccalaureate

career   occupation for which a worker receives training and has an opportunity for advancement

certified   approved as meeting established requirements for skill, knowledge, and experience in a particular field; people are certified by the organization of professionals in their field

college   higher education institution that is above the high school level

community college   public two-year college attended by students who do not usually live at the college; a graduate of a community college receives an associate's degree and may transfer to a four-year college or university to complete a bachelor's degree

diploma   certificate or document given by a school to show that a person has completed a course or has graduated from the school

distance education   type of educational program that allows students to take classes and complete their education by mail or the Internet

doctorate   highest academic rank or title granted by a graduate school to a person who has completed a two- to three-year program after having received a master's degree

fringe benefit   payment or benefit to an employee in addition to regular wages or salary; examples of fringe benefits include a pension, a paid vacation, and health or life insurance

graduate school   school that people may attend after they have received their bachelor's degree; people who complete an educational program at a graduate school earn a master's degree or a doctorate

intern   advanced student (usually one with at least some college training) who is employed in a job that is intended to provide supervised practical career experience

internship   (1) the position or job of an intern; (2) period of time when a person is an intern

junior college   two-year college that offers courses like those in the first half of a four-year college program; graduates of a junior college usually receive an associate's degree and may transfer to a four-year college or university to complete a bachelor's degree

liberal arts   subjects covered by college courses that develop broad general knowledge rather than specific occupational skills; the liberal arts are often considered to include philosophy, literature and the arts, history, language, and some courses in the social sciences and natural sciences

major (in college)   academic field in which a student specializes and receives a degree

Glossary

master's degree academic rank or title granted by a graduate school to a person who has completed a one- or two-year program after having received a bachelor's degree

online education academic study that is performed by using a computer and the Internet

pension amount of money paid regularly by an employer to a former employee after he or she retires from working

scholarship gift of money to a student to help the student pay for further education

social studies courses of study (such as civics, geography, and history) that deal with how human societies work

starting salary salary paid to a newly hired employee; the starting salary is usually a smaller amount than is paid to a more experienced worker

technical college private or public college offering two- or four-year programs in technical subjects; technical colleges offer courses in both general and technical subjects and award associate's degrees and bachelor's degrees

undergraduate student at a college or university who has not yet received a degree

undergraduate degree see **bachelor's degree**

union organization whose members are workers in a particular industry or company; the union works to gain better wages, benefits, and working conditions for its members; also called a labor union or trade union

wage money that is paid in return for work done, especially money paid on the basis of the number of hours or days worked

Index of Job Titles

A
acquisitions editors 17
advertising and marketing managers 7
advertising and marketing workers 5–8
advertising sales executives 5
advertising workers 5–8
aerial photographers 54
art directors 9–12
assistant editors 46
associate editors 45
authors' agents 41–44

B
bindery workers 13–16
biographers 81
book editors 17–20

C
camera operators 57
columnists 21–24, 66, 81
comedy writers 81
commercial photographers 54
compositors 57
content editors 17
copy editors 17, 46, 50
copywriters 82
correspondents 65
creative writers 81–82
critics 81

D
department editors 50
desktop publishing specialists 25–28, 57–58

E
editorial writers 66
editor in chief 49
essayists 81

F
fact checkers 19, 46
fashion illustrators 34
feature writers 65–66
film strippers 57
fine art photographers 54

G
graphic designers 29–32

I
illustrators 33–36
indexers 37–40

L
line editors 17, 19
literary agents 41–44
lithographers 57

M
magazine editors 45–48
managing editors 46, 49
marketing workers 5–8

89

media buyers 5
medical illustrators 33–34

N
natural science illustrators 34
news editors 50
newspaper editors 49–52, 66
newswriters 81
novelists 81, 83

O
online editors 50

P
paste-up workers 57
photographers 53–56
photojournalists 54, 55
platemakers 57
playwrights 82, 83
poets 81, 83
portrait photographers 54
pre-flight technicians 58
prepress workers 57–60
printing press operators 61–64
printing press workers 61–64
production editors 19, 46, 50
proofreaders 18, 19
public information officers 69

R
reporters 65–68
researchers 46

S
scanner operators 58
science and medical writers 69–72
scientific photographers 54
screenwriters 82
scriptwriters 82
senior or executive editors 45
short story writers 81, 83
stitcher operators 14
story editors 49
syndicated news columnists 66

T
technical writers and editors 73–76, 83
topical reporters 65
typesetters 57

W
webmasters 77–80
wire editors 49
writers 81–84
writers' representatives 41–44

Browse and Learn More

Books

Brogan, Kathryn S., ed. *2004 Writer's Market*. Cincinnati, Ohio: Writers Digest Books, 2003.

Camenson, Blythe. *Careers in Publishing*. New York: McGraw-Hill/Contemporary Books, 2002.

Degalan, Julie, and Stephen Lambert. *Great Jobs for English Majors*. 2nd ed. New York: McGraw-Hill/Contemporary Books, 2000.

Johansson, Kaj, Peter Lundberg, and Robert Ryberg. *A Guide to Graphic Print Production*. Hoboken, N.J.: Wiley, 2002.

Olmert, Michael. *The Smithsonian Book of Books*. Washington, D.C.: Smithsonian Institution Press, 2003.

Rhatigan, Joe. *In Print!: 40 Cool Publishing Projects for Kids*. Asheville, N.C.: Lark Books, 2003.

Zackheim, Sarah Parsons, and Adrian Zackheim. *Getting Your Book Published For Dummies*. Hoboken, N.J.: Wiley, 2000.

Websites

Association of American Publishers
http://www.publishers.org

Authorlink
http://www.authorlink.com/index.html

Books A to Z
http://booksatoz.com

BookWeb.org
http://www.ambook.org

BookWire
http://www.bookwire.com/bookwire

Creative Writing for Teens
http://kidswriting.about.com

KidPub
http://www.kidpub.org/kidpub

Kids Who Read
http://kwr.co-nect.net

Kidscribe: A Bilingual Site for Kid Authors
http://web2.airmail.net/def

Magazine Publishers of America
http://www.magazine.org

Publishers Weekly
http://www.publishersweekly.com

Publishing Central
http://www.publishingcentral.com

The Rainwater Press Publishing Primer (glossary of publishing terms)
http://www.rainwater.com/glossary.html

Young Writer
http://www.mystworld.com/youngwriter

The Zuzu Kids Page
http://www.zuzu.com/kidlink.htm

LEMOORE STACKS
31965000324498
070.5023 DIS
Discovering careers for your

DATE DUE

GAYLORD		PRINTED IN U.S.A.

WEST HILLS COLLEGE
LEMOORE LIBRARY/LRC